THE
INTERRUPTED
TRAVELER

A Novel

A.D. Plautz

SCRIPTOR HOUSE
The Epitome of Greatness

Scriptor House LLC

2810 N Church St Wilmington, Delaware, 19802

www.scriptorhouse.com

Phone: +1302-205-2043

Paperback: 979-8-88692-008-6
eBook: 979-8-88692-009-3

Review of The Interrupted Traveler

Readers of this smart, lively yarn will enjoy watching an ordinary guy show how extraordinary he can be with the right challenges. On a sad family errand to the South Pacific, Ron Pritchard must first survive a plane crash on a remote, uninhabited island, then look after the other survivors – a hot pop star and her entourage – while waiting for rescuers. But a vicious crew of drug smugglers is also searching for the lost plane… Each new crisis forces Ron to analyze cooly but empathize passionately. This book is a genuine, compulsive page-turner.

-Joe Sanders, veteran thriller reviewer for *Publishers Weekly*

Note: Any and all of the characters and persons in this story are totally fictitious with no relation to any actual persons, living or dead.

Chapter 1
December

Ron Pritchard was sitting in his living room. He was 53 years old and still had blond hair, although it was starting to turn gray. He had gained some weight over the years and was pushing close to 200 pounds. Not that bad, considering he was six feet tall. He looked out the front room window. The late December snow was falling slowly outside. The ground in the front yard was still too warm to allow accumulation, so the snow was melting as it landed. It was a cold December day and Ron was very tired. It had been a very long day. He looked at the kitchen table with the box holding the urn. The memorial service went pretty well, he thought. His wife had been very active in the church and almost everyone in the congregation had turned out for the service. He had read a short eulogy about how she had been a successful teacher and the light of his life. But afterward at the reception it was awkward as everyone expressed their sorrow at her passing. He just wanted to be away and be alone, so he had left the reception early. He just wanted to be away from all of those people. But now it really hit him. She was gone. Really gone. The light of his life, his wife, his soul mate, was gone. He looked at the whiskey bottle on the desk. He could crawl into that and the numbness might help relieve his pain. But he thought, no, that was not the answer.

He had met her in college, and after a few dates they had fallen in love. They had lived through some difficult experiences during their college courtship

ut had emerged totally committed to each other. They had been married
or twenty-four years. It was rough in the beginning but they had emerged
ok. They had struggled at first to buy a house and raise two daughters. She
had never complained during the hard times. It was strange, he thought,
she never got sick, was always nursing him and the two girls though colds
and the flu and the pandemic. They had talked for years about going to the
South Seas for an extended vacation to Tahiti and enjoying life. There was
always something preventing them, either he was traveling for engineering
conferences, or she was busy teaching art classes in the local high school.
Now that they could really afford it, they had finally put money down for the
long awaited vacation trip. Both of their daughters had left home, one had
an apartment and worked as a nurse's aide at the Cleveland Clinic; the
other had met her love, got married and was living in Oregon.

His wife Susan had always wanted to go to Tahiti and had tons of
brochures for the luxury resorts on Bora Bora. They finally scheduled the
trip for mid-March to coincide with their twenty-fifth anniversary. Susan
always planned far ahead to get the best deals. A month after they made
the down payment for the trip, she noticed a small lump in her breast. A
trip to the doctor revealed bad news: she had stage four breast cancer. The
doctors started her on typical chemotherapy and radiation treatments. She
would come home and be sick for a couple of days after each treatment. The
doctors were optimistic about the treatment, but nothing worked. They had
considered an operation but it was already spreading too fast. She cried a
lot from the pain but still wanted to visit Tahiti before she died. The cancer
ate her up so quickly even the doctors were surprised. Four and a half weeks
after the initial diagnosis she was gone. Now he was alone in the big house
they had purchased 23 years ago when she was pregnant with their first
daughter.

The doorbell rang. He got up and walked to the front door. His old college buddy, George Coleman was standing on the top step. He was dressed in a blue police uniform. Ron had seen him briefly at the reception but did not get a chance to talk with him other than say hello.

"Hi, Ron, you left the reception early; I thought I would stop and see if you were ok." Ron moved aside to let him into the front room and closed the door.

"I wasn't that close with all of those church people. I just wanted to come home." Ron replied.

"I thought you might want some company." George held up a bag with a six pack of beer. "Care to have a beer?"

"Yeah, I guess so." Ron moved the urn to the kitchen counter and got a couple of beer mugs out of the cabinet. They moved to the kitchen table. "I'm glad you were able to make it to the service," Ron said.

"I wouldn't miss it. I know how Susan and you got together in college. I never saw two people more in love." George had been the campus police chief at the time and remembered the drama of that first summer. Ron had assisted the police department in tracking down and arresting a campus rapist that had attacked Susan. "You were my best friend back then."

"Yeah, those were interesting days." Ron poured beer for George and himself in a couple of mugs. "So, what are you doing these days? We haven't seen you for a couple of years." George had been his best man when he married Sue, and Ron had returned the favor by being George's best man when he had married Jennifer.

"If you remember, I was the police chief in our old college town, but I currently have an offer to join the Cleveland Police as a detective," George replied.

"Wow. You're moving here to Cleveland?" Ron was glad for his friend.

"Yeah, Jenny is happy to come to the big city." Jenny was George's wife. "She couldn't make the trip up here today, too busy in her flower shop."

"I am happy for you. Maybe we can get together more often." Ron took a swallow of beer.

"So… what are you going to do now?" George asked.

"I have some accumulated vacation time I was saving up for a trip with Sue, but now I guess I will go by myself." Ron looked at the urn on the counter.

"You're going on vacation?" George looked at him over the beer stein.

"One of the last things Susan said to me was that she wanted to go to Tahiti and be on the beach. So, I intend to take her ashes there and spread them on the beach." Ron choked up a bit and a tear ran down his cheek.

"Wow. They let you do that?"

"I don't care. I'm going to do it." Ron looked away, brushing aside the tear drop. "Well, are you going to travel alone?" George asked.

"Yeah, just to go and be there for a week. Then come right back. Then I want to get back to work and get busy to escape the sorrow."

"When are you going?"

"Well, we originally were going to go in March for our anniversary but I am going to trade in the tickets and go sooner and get away from the winter snow. Maybe go in early February."

"Good choice. I would go with you but I have to start with the Cleveland Police department next month." George finished his beer. "I probably won't get much vacation the first year."

"That's ok. I probably wouldn't be real good company anyway," Ron replied.

"Are you still working at the aerospace company?" George decided to change subjects.

"Yeah, I worked my way up to be principal engineer. They wanted me to be a manager of the engineering department but I turned them down. Let someone else worry about schedules and personnel problems," Ron replied.

"Do you have any health problems from the bad auto wreck?" George asked. He remembered the severe car accident the summer before Ron graduated from college.

"I used to have a lot of pain in my leg where it got smashed, but my doctor got me into swimming therapy," Ron explained. "I go twice a week and it really helps. I have become a pretty good swimmer now." Ron noted with some pride. "I also started to take flying lessons in a piper cub at the county airport but I stopped when Sue got sick."

"That is so cool. How far did you get?" George asked.

"Only had two lessons so far but yes, it was pretty cool." Ron smiled. "I didn't see any Corvettes in your driveway. You still drive one?"

"No. After the kids came along it did not seem to be much of a family car so I traded it in on a Honda. Not as much fun to drive but a lot more practical." Ron took a sip of beer and wondered what he would do with Susan's old Toyota. Maybe trade it in for something just a little bit sportier he thought. He would now have room in the garage for a Corvette.

They had another beer but then George had to leave. He didn't want to get home too late and it would not do his future police career any good to get a DUI. They said their good byes and George left. Ron looked again at the whiskey bottle, picked it up but then put it away. He decided to go to bed and started to turn out the lights.

The doorbell rang again. Ron went to the door. His two daughters Sandra and Alice were standing there.

"Come on in," he opened the door wider.

"We thought we would stop by," Alice said. Both she and her sister Sandra looked like they had been crying. They both turned to hug Ron. They had cried throughout most of the funeral service at the church. Both had had a special relationship with their mother.

"Sorry I did not stay long for the reception," Ron said.

"How are we going live without mom?" Sandra sobbed. She talked with her mother daily about her problems at work and Sue always had a solution for her.

"We will just have to keep on living the best we can," Ron replied. "She would have wanted us to do that." Ron recalled that when they were growing up in the house he had often felt like an outsider. The two daughters and their mother were always in their own little group doing things together and he always seemed to be on the outside while they were growing up. Since he was typically always traveling on business it seemed normal for the girls and Sue to band together. His wife had raised both of the girls right. There was very little sibling rivalry between them. They all shared among themselves unselfishly. Susan had seen to that. That stopped when she became sick. She hid the cancer from the girls as long as possible. Then when she became so sick she couldn't hide it anymore she finally confided in them. So, her death was pretty much a sudden shock to them. They stayed for a while and talked about their mother and reminisced about some stories before they left. Ron invited them to stay the night at the house but both had other plans, so they left after giving him hugs. Ron was really tired now. He turned out the lights, locked the door and went to bed. The big old house was sort of lonely now. As he lay in bed he started thinking maybe he would sell the house and get a condo. This house had memories of Sue everywhere. He really did not know what to do. She had decorated the house to her preferences as he seldom had much to say about anything she wanted. He finally fell into a fitful sleep.

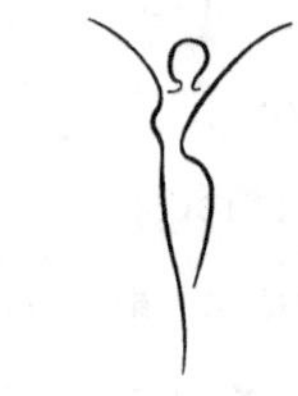

CHAPTER 2
JANUARY

Ron had accumulated enough vacation time to take two weeks off from work so he sat down and figured out his travel Itinerary. He would fly from Cleveland to Chicago, and from there to San Francisco. After a short layover he would catch a flight to Hawaii and then to Papeete, Tahiti in French Polynesia. From there it was a short flight to Bora Bora where the tourist resorts were. It was a total of five flights and about 16 hours flying time, and that did not include the time between connecting flights. So, he figured he would take almost two days of travel time from Cleveland. He had the AAA book his stay in Bora Bora for one week starting 2 days after he left Cleveland. He had reviewed the travel brochures that his wife had accumulated. She had marked The Intercontinental Resort as her first choice. It was a five-star hotel and restaurant in Bora Bora, so he had the Triple A also book that resort. It was going to be tight to meet all of the connections but it should work. It was very expensive but he did not care. Since he had canceled his wife's fare, it was significantly less cost for him to travel alone. The initial travel date was somewhat fluid but everything did fit into the end of the second week in February. He scheduled his vacation for that time even though it conflicted with the timing of the project he was working on. His boss at work was not happy with the timing but knew that Ron was still suffering from the loss of his wife. Since December, Ron had worked 12-hour days to get the project going and it was slightly ahead of schedule, so his boss could not deny Ron the vacation request. The extra time at work helped to keep him so busy he did not have time to dwell on his wife's passing. He would go to work early and work late. Then he would come home, fix supper, do the dishes, watch the news and then go to bed. He typically drank a beer with supper but otherwise did not resort to drinking. The pastor of the church visited him on a Saturday afternoon to ask how he was doing since he had not been attending church. He typically went to church with his wife but never officially joined the church as a member. He enjoyed the sermons but did not see any sense in going to church alone. They had a meaningful talk about surviving the loss of a spouse. Ron told the Pastor he was having some difficulty accepting the loss of his wife but was ok. The pastor sort of understood this and told him if he ever needed any counseling to call him.

CHAPTER 3
FEBRUARY

As Ron packed for the trip to Tahiti, he put the funeral urn which was a tightly sealed stainless steel container in his check-in bag. He knew better than to try to explain to the TSA checkers that it was not a bomb of some sort. As it was, he still had to fill out some paperwork for transporting a body, even though it was only the ashes. He had to lie about why he was transporting the body but the clerk did not question him about it. (He said he was returning the body to be buried in her home land). He just hoped that his checked-in baggage was not lost during the trip somehow. So, he had the one small black suitcase and a carry-on bag with three changes of clothes. He had packed two novels to read on the plane and three or four energy snack bars. He included his travel kit with shaving stuff and a few vitamin pills and other pills (for headaches and diarrhea) in the carry-on bag. He had the mail stopped by the Post Office and canceled the morning paper for two weeks. He was only planning to be gone for a week but he had learned the hard way that often times flights were cancelled or delayed.

The trip to Cleveland Hopkins Airport was uneventful. Although it had snowed the previous night, the roads were mostly clear and it was a short trip from his house in Strongsville to the airport. He parked his Honda in the Park and Fly parking garage and boarded the bus to the airport. Some flights were being cancelled due to the snowy weather – he hoped his was still on schedule. After checking his suitcase with the urn at the service desk, he inquired about his flight status. The attendant noted that it was delayed but not cancelled. He went to the TSA check point. He passed through without any difficulty since his passport was current. His carry-on bag passed through the x-ray machine with no trouble. He went to the gate to wait for the plane to arrive. Although it was late, the flight did eventually arrive and he boarded. He had purchased first class seats all the way to Tahiti. He hated to be cramped and was used to traveling in business class for his company. He had the extra funds available from cancelling his wife's travel tickets, so why not? He arrived in Chicago about an hour late and almost missed the connecting flight to San Francisco. The gates were on opposite sides of the airport so he had no time to grab a meal but had to rush to the gate and caught the flight to Hawaii without any problems. In Hawaii he was finally able to get a meal in the airport since he had some time before his flight to Tahiti. He got on the plane ok and just got settled in when the pilot came on the intercom and noted that they might be delayed for takeoff since some minor repairs had to be done to the aircraft. So, the flight to French Polynesia was delayed due to some aircraft problems, and it sat on the tarmac in Oahu for several hours after boarding was completed so that repairs could be performed. Ron did some calculating and if they did not leave soon he would miss the final leg of the trip, the commuter flight from Papeete to Bora Bora, and might be stuck in Papeete. The pilot came on the intercom and reported that the airport technicians were almost done and that they would be taking off soon. Ron did not mind being stuck in Tahiti for a day, but he did not want to miss his check-in time at the Intercontinental Resort on Bora Bora. He hoped that they would depart pretty quickly. An hour later they were still waiting and some of the passengers were complaining to the flight attendant about the delay. She could do nothing but started to pass out some snacks and drinks to the people. The plane was almost full with only a few empty seats. Ron knew it would not help to complain. He had flown on enough business trips to know that this type of delay was common. Finally, the repair work was completed and the aircraft took off, 3 hours late. It would be almost impossible to meet the flight from Papeete to Bora Bora, but there was a slim chance.

CHAPTER 4
DAY 1   1:00 PM

Teddy Cooper was walking toward the aircraft arrival at Papeete from Hong Kong. Teddy was an older man about 60, dressed in a blue shirt with pilot wings pinned to the pocket and worn blue jeans. He had his captain's cap on. He was a bit scruffy with a beard, seriously overweight and smoked too much. He ran 'Cooper's Charters.' It was a small single aircraft operation out of Papeete airport that specialized in short hops to Bora Bora and back. The aircraft he was looking at was just in from Hong Kong and was a large 767. He knew the company technician for this aircraft and had made a deal with him. Today, Teddy was doing something illegal. He was going to receive a special package that was hidden in the landing gear well of the 767. The company technician, a guy he only knew as "Bobby" was dressed in technician's overalls and met him on the tarmac as the huge 767 pulled up to the gate. Before any other airport personnel could get to the plane, Bobby pushed his tool cart over to the right main landing gear and appeared to be inspecting the gear. He reached up and retrieved two packages, white plastic-covered bags, and calmly stuffed them into his tool cart and slid the drawer on the cart closed. He then walked over and inspected the other landing gears before he pushed his cart back toward the hanger where Teddy was waiting. They both entered the hanger where Cooper kept his aircraft, an old Mallard G73 amphibian aircraft. Cooper gave Bobby a thick envelope with cash in it and took the two packages. It was a total of eight kilos of pure uncut heroin, worth over a hundred thousand dollars. He looked around but no one had seen the exchange. Bobby walked back to his aircraft, pushing his service cart. Teddy hummed as he calmly strolled over to his aircraft. He opened the storage compartment he typically used to carry passenger luggage. He looked around but no one was watching. He stored the packages in a black garbage bag and pushed it all way in the back of the compartment and then covered it with a sheet of black plastic. Teddy smiled. This was one way of getting around the island police and customs officials. His customer, Snake Caputo, would be happy. They had had this arrangement for several months now and it was much more profitable than the income from the charter. He would fly toward Bora Bora and then divert and land in the water at Tupai, an uninhabited atoll about twenty miles north of Bora Bora and make the exchange to Snake's large 56-foot cabin cruiser yacht. Teddy did not know or care what Caputo did with the stuff. He simply collected 5,000 Tahitian francs for each delivery trip. There was very little risk in the whole business. He knew better than to double cross Caputo, who ran the rackets in Tahiti and had several violent men in place throughout the islands, most of these men were very bad and all carried guns. He typically did not take charter customers on these trips but lately he had decided to increase his profit by taking paying customers. He would use the excuse of letting the charter customers see the tourist stop of Tupai while he did some minor engine maintenance. Tupai was a protected nature preserve for sea turtles and exotic birds. Visits and tours had to be approved by the Bora Bora visitor's bureau but he could always claim engine trouble if he was caught. Caputo did not like this but he tolerated it. The drug shipments were only about once a month so he did not have to make the delivery that often. He looked around and was satisfied that no one had seen the exchange. That was good. He knew that if he was caught, Caputo would have him killed. The previous competitor charter aircraft pilot, had run afoul of Caputo and then had disappeared, plane and all. So now Teddy had gotten the same deal from Caputo and did not want to screw it up. It was also nice that he didn't have any competition now and could charge higher prices for a charter flight. He walked out of the hanger and lit up a cigarette. Then he walked to the pilot access door to the Tahiti Faa'a airport entrance. After he was screened by the TSA representative, he made it to his charter flight desk. Suzy Kwan was his pretty Oriental assistant who manned the desk when he was away. Typically, most people used the regularly scheduled commuter flights from Papeete to the Moto-Muti Airport on Bora Bora. But occasionally he had a customer or two since he was the now the only charter business available.

"We have any customers today?" Teddy asked Suzy. Suzy Kwan was a young Oriental girl in her twenties, wearing a white mini skirt, blue sleeveless halter top blouse and sneakers. She had only had the job for a few months, but she was valuable since she spoke both French and English and was sort of attractive. She was sitting behind the desk, texting with her sister on her phone.

"Non," she responded in French.

"Well, let me know if any show up. I'll be in the café lounge." The lounge was across the aisle from the charter desk. He went in and sat down and ordered a cheeseburger, fries and a beer. The pain in his shoulder came back again as he waited for his food. He probably should see a doctor about it but the pain went away and he soon forgot it. He ordered another beer and was just finishing it when his cell phone rang. It was Caputo.

"Everything ok?" the gruff voice asked.

"No problem. Be at the same place?" Teddy asked. "Yes. Don't be late." He hung up.

Teddy put the phone away. This deal was really good, he thought. He only paid the service technician Bobby one thousand Tahitian francs so he made a nice profit. He thought about the flight today. It was a clear sky with a few scattered clouds. There should be no problem filing a flight plan to Bora Bora. Half way there he would change course for Tupai, telling traffic control he was going to put down in the lagoon and check his engine. He would often let his customers visit the uninhabited, pristine island atoll when he had passengers. Typically, one was supposed to file a request with the Environmental officials to visit the island in advance, but the traffic controllers did not care about that. After making the exchange with Caputo he would fly to Bora Bora and customs would inspect his aircraft but not find anything. A tropical storm was predicted for later in the evening but he would be back from Bora Bora way before then. The pain in his shoulder got worse but he ordered another beer anyway. He would normally have had a heavier vodka drink to make the pain go away but since he had to fly, he stuck with the beer. He would not even be flying today if he did not have the special cargo. It sure would be nice to have some customers to take along to increase his profit. He looked around to find a place to light a cigarette.

CHAPTER 5
DAY 1   2:15 PM

Taylor Smith fidgeted in her seat. Her special charter jet aircraft was supposed to land at Papeete and refuel before taking off for Bora Bora where the film crew was waiting to shoot the new music video for her latest album. Now the pilot announced that he was having trouble with the starboard engine of their two-engine Gulfstream 280 aircraft. It was an eight passenger luxury aircraft but only held five passengers; her mother Sara, her best friend Betty, her agent Sylvia, her bodyguard Stanley and herself. She was used to traveling in comfort and the charter company promised they would get her to Bora Bora on time for the scheduled shoot. Now the pilot was saying they would probably have to be delayed at Papeete until the engine could be serviced. She partially blamed herself since the visit to Tahiti to do the photo shoot was her decision. She had figured that it would be a nice vacation for her after the shoot, to be able to just relax for a couple of weeks. She had worked hard all autumn on the new album and wanted to have some free time to hit the beach. They could have filmed it in Los Angeles or Hawaii but she wanted to go someplace where she would not be bombarded by the press or her fans. So, she told her film crew that they were going to do the shoot in Tahiti. Her agent Sylvia had complained that it would delay the production schedule and cost almost twice as much, but Taylor was the boss and no one argued with her. She was recently separated from her boyfriend so she wanted to get away from the news hounds and paparazzi that constantly followed and photographed her wherever she went. Her father had passed away suddenly last summer and she wanted to get her mother out of the house and hopefully enjoy a nice quiet vacation in the best resort in Bora Bora.

After the pilot made his announcement, Taylor asked the stewardess if she would ask the pilot how long the delay would be in Papeete. The stewardess went up to talk to the pilot and came back a few minutes later.

"He said that he may have to shut down the engine, it is overheating and losing thrust."

The stewardess was a young brunette in a company uniform. Her name tag said Helen. She was amazed to be talking to Taylor Smith, who was one of her favorite pop star singers. "We don't know how long it will take to fix it. As it is, we will be delayed in landing if he shuts down the engine."

"Can this plane fly with only one engine?" Taylor asked, becoming concerned.

She could only see vast expanse of blue ocean water out of the aircraft window.

"Yes. There is no problem with that. It will reduce our speed but that is all," the stewardess replied. The plane was qualified to fly on only one engine, but the stewardess was herself becoming concerned, though she could not let her passengers see this. The stewardess was new to the charter aircraft company but had agreed to work this flight since there would be a long layover in Tahiti. It appeared now that the layover would be a lot longer if they had to make repairs to the plane. She figured that as long as the company was paying her expenses she might as well enjoy the time in Tahiti. She had never been to the tropics so she had signed up for this trip. Most of the other girls had turned down the trip since it was a long one.

CHAPTER 6
DAY 1   3:10 PM

Ron Pritchard looked out the aircraft window. Finally, they were over Tahiti. He could see the lush tropical forest and mountains below as the 737 crossed the large island to the Papeete airport on the western side of the island. He checked his map to look at the island chain again.

There were a lot of islands he thought. But he was really only interested in getting to Bora Bora. That was where the tourist resort he was going to was located. It was only supposed to be about a 30 minute flight from Papeete to the much smaller airport on Bora Bora and it was already late in the afternoon. There were actually only three commuter flights to Bora Bora per day and his calculations, adjusted for time change, showed that he had probably missed the last connecting flight by about a half hour. He might have to stay in one of the hotels near the airport until tomorrow, he thought. He hoped that the expensive resort on Bora Bora would hold his reservation.

He would have to call to make sure. The languages on Tahiti were *Reo Tahiti* and French. Not many people spoke English although he was sure that since there were many tourists from the states that probably visited the islands, some of the people should speak English. He had some high school French but was sure that he would not be able to converse adequately with what little he remembered. He dug out a French – English dictionary from his carry-on bag and thumbed through it. If he had one of those fancy smart phones it could be used to translate languages easily but he had forgotten to add that App. It was too late now.

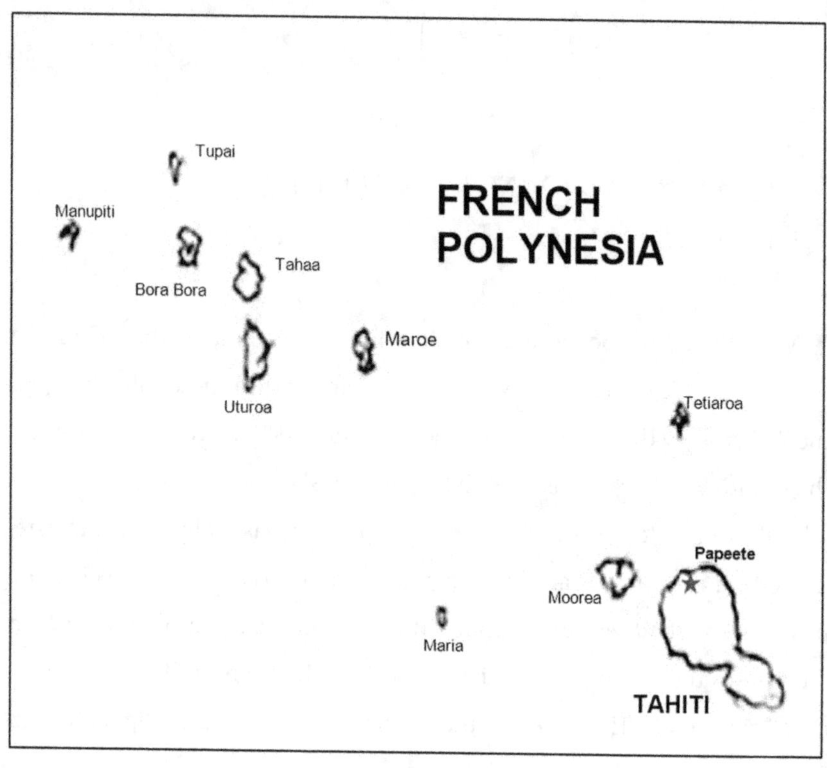

The plane landed without any problem and taxied up to the terminal. The announcement was in French and he could not translate all of it but he had traveled a lot and figured it was the standard arrival information. He did catch that the outside temperature was 30 degrees Celsius (about 88 degrees F). So, it was fairly hot here, something that was typical of an island this close to the equator. Ron left the aircraft and walked down the airport terminal. There were a couple of shops and restaurants, but nothing as glitzy as the airports he was used to in the states. A few people were walking around, but the airport was almost deserted. He checked the video monitor for flight information. His scheduled flight on the small commuter plane had already left. He walked over to the airline information desk and tried to get an attendant's attention.

"Qu'est-ce que c'est?" (*What do you want?*) The woman behind the counter asked him, looking up from her computer screen.

"Can you help me? I believe I missed the flight to Bora Bora." Ron asked helplessly.

"Oh. You come een on thee last flight?" The woman said slowly with a heavy French accent.

"Yes. Is there another commuter flight?" Ron was hopeful. He showed her his ticket and boarding pass.

"Non. Thee next flight to Bora Bora ees tomorrow." She noted that he was disappointed. "Eeff you wanna get Bora Bora today, there ees a charter flight company down the terminal near by the baggage claim." She pointed at the stairs.

"Ok. Thanks." He did not know what to do. He really wanted to get to the resort today or he might lose his reservation. He walked over to a seating area and took out his cell phone. He punched in the number for the resort but his phone said no service. He thought about using a pay phone to call the AAA trip service number back in the states, but it would be almost midnight now in Ohio. Maybe he could use the pay phone to check his reservation. Or...he could check out the inter-island charter. He got up and went down the stairs. The charter desk had an attractive Asian girl behind it playing with her cell phone. The sign overhead said 'Cooper's Charters.'

"Hello," he said, smiling, hoping that she spoke English. "Yes?" she answered. "Are you interested in a charter flight?"

"Does it go to Bora Bora?" he asked desperately, noting that advertisements for the Bora Bora resorts were posted on the wall behind her.

"Yes, we have one flight going today to Bora Bora in about 45 minutes." She smiled at him. "Sometimes the flight from Hawaii comes in late and we are the only option to get to that tourist island until tomorrow."

"How much does it cost?" he asked.

"It is a short flight but it will cost you 150 francs." She knew that Teddy would be happy that another American tourist was stranded again. Normally it would be a married couple, but this man was by himself.

"That seems like a lot." Ron replied. He thought maybe he could bargain with her for a lower fare.

"Take it or leave it." She turned her attention back to her cell phone.

"Ok. I'll take it. But I have to get my baggage from the baggage claim." He realized she wasn't going to budge on the price. She probably had dealt with Americans before. He walked over to the baggage claim to get his suitcase. He was relieved that his suitcase with the funeral urn in it had made it this far without getting lost. He had to go through customs but the officer there was sort of bored and did not ask an American tourist many questions. When he got back to the charter desk, he saw an unshaven, overweight man in a pilot hat standing at the desk talking to the desk clerk. Ron walked up and said hello. Teddy looked over at him.

"Hello. So, you want to go to Bora Bora?" Teddy turned and smiled at him with discolored yellow teeth. He also had bad breath so Ron stepped back a little.

"Yes." Ron said. "Are you an American?" He was hoping this was not the charter

"Yeah, I have been flying in these islands for the past 25 years. I am Teddy Cooper, your pilot." Teddy pointed to the desk clerk. "Pay the fee and I will put you on board." Ron paid the girl with a Visa card who then gave him a small ticket and a brochure for Cooper's Charters.

Teddy took him through a side door to an adjacent hanger. Ron carried his bags and then looked at the plane. It was an old two-engine propeller aircraft but had long floats on the edges of the wings. The landing gears protruded from the main fuselage. He looked at the floats and realized that this thing could land on land or water. At least if they had engine trouble over water, he wouldn't have to swim for it.

"This is your plane?" Ron was horrified. It looked like it badly needed maintenance.

Teddy looked at him. "She may be old but she still gets around the islands ok." "It looks like something left over from World War II." Ron commented.

"You are close. This old G73 Mallard was built in 1948. Here, let me stow your bag." He took Ron's suitcase over to a hatch near the rear of the plane and put it in. "You might as well get inside. We will take off in about fifteen minutes." He pointed to the stair steps going up to the open hatch on the port side of the aircraft. Teddy was glad to have a passenger; it would help cover the cost of fuel for the trip. Just then Teddy's cell phone rang. He moved away to the hanger entrance to talk.

As Ron got on board he noticed there was a single aisle with single seats on either side of the aircraft and it only had 10 seats. The seats were badly in need of re- upholstering, but since he was only going to go for a 30 minute ride, he supposed it would be ok. He sat down in the third seat from the front in one of the least offensive looking seats. He noticed there weren't any seat belts but every other seat had a life preserver under it. They looked like old World War two vintage Mae Wests. *What have I gotten myself into?* he thought to himself. He wondered why the charter plane was even going to Bora Bora if there were no other passengers before he bought his ticket. Teddy must also be carrying some cargo he thought.

Grumman G73 Mallard

CHAPTER 7
DAY 1   3:15 PM

Taylor Smith looked out the window as the Gulfstream 280 landed on the runway without difficulty. They had finally landed at Papeete. The pilot had to shut down the starboard engine fifteen minutes before landing, but since they were so close to landing he did not radio the control tower that they needed an emergency landing. The plane was handling perfectly. His charter company did not need the bad publicity that an emergency landing might bring to his company and the aircraft landed without any issues. They taxied up to the terminal. There was no jet way configuration for a Gulfstream aircraft so the co-pilot had to let down the internal folding stairway for everyone to depart. The co-pilot then went out and walked back to look at the bad engine.

The burst of hot air hit Taylor Smith in the face. She was wearing a light pink blouse and red shorts but started to perspire immediately. *Wow. It was really hot here,* she thought to herself. The pilot came back out of the cockpit and looked at his passengers. "I am not sure how long we will be here, so you all might just as well go inside the terminal."

"Do we have to go through customs?" Stanley the bodyguard asked. He was afraid they would confiscate his revolver. He had a license for it but wasn't sure it would be acceptable out here. The officials in Bora Bora had already accepted his gun permit.

"No, just go to the first floor staging area while I check the engine problem." He watched the five customers walk toward the terminal. This was not going to be very good if they had a long layover. His exclusive charter company did not have a maintenance facility in the mid-Pacific. He walked over to the co-pilot. The co-pilot was not smiling.

"Bad news….the compressor stage has lost a blade and it went into one of the combustor cans. We are just lucky we got here ok without a turbine failure or an engine fire." The co-pilot pointed to the engine. "If it had entered the turbine stage, we would have had an engine fire. We are just lucky, I guess," the co-pilot informed him.

"Aw shit," the pilot said. "That means a total engine replacement. That could take several days or even a week." He knew they would have to ship him a new engine from California. And also, a repair crew to do the work. He turned and went back into the terminal. He would be stuck here for at least a week. *Oh well, there were worse places to have downtime,* he thought. He saw his five customers sitting in the waiting area. At least it was air conditioned in there he thought. He walked over to Stanley. "Sorry folks. We need an engine replacement and will be down for at least a week."

"Oh no…." Taylor Smith said loudly. "How are we going to get to our film shoot?"

Her agent Sylvia stood up and said "We cannot miss this photo shoot. We cannot tie up the production crew; it will cost too much. We have to find another way of getting to Bora Bora," she exclaimed, frowning at the pilot.

"Sorry folks, there is nothing I can do," the pilot explained.

"Can you fly us to Bora Bora on one engine?" Sylvia asked desperately.

"No….I can't take that chance. I would lose my license." The pilot turned and walked back outside to see about getting their luggage off the plane.

"What are we going to do?" Sylvia screamed after him.

Taylor's mother, Sara, calmly replied, "We probably could find a boat or charter to take us there." She had been looking at the posters on the wall. One of them was about a company called Cooper's Air Charters. She pointed to the sign.

"Ok. Let's do that." Taylor said. She wanted to get to the island resort as soon as possible.

A few minutes later the group of five people lined up in front of the Cooper's Charters desk. The four women and Stanley, who was pushing a cart stacked high with the women's luggage, all looked hopefully at Suzy Kwan.

"Yes, we do have a charter aircraft that is going to Bora Bora... but it is about to take off." Suzy explained to them. Then she saw Taylor Smith and recognized her. "Wait, let me call to see if it has left yet." She turned and walked into the back room and called Teddy on her cell phone. "You won't believe who needs a trip to Bora Bora!" she exclaimed.

"Who?" Teddy was immediately interested if he could get more additional fares for the trip.

"It's Taylor Smith!" Suzy excitedly exclaimed. "So, who is Taylor Smith?" Teddy was confused. "She is a famous pop star singer!"

"Is she rich?" He asked.

"She's probably worth several million francs," Suzy replied.

"Well, then….sell her a ticket!" Teddy said, his mind already working fast. "She has four people with her," Suzy replied.

"Ok. That is even more money. I will see you get a bonus.

Suzy returned to the front desk. "You're in luck. He hasn't left yet. There is still time to board."

"Oh, thank God." Silvia sighed. "We can still make it on time."

They purchased five tickets and waited for the pilot to come and get them.

Teddy was still in the hanger. His first passenger was already on board. He walked over to the door of the hanger and called Snake Caputo on his satellite cell phone.

"What?" Caputo was irritated by Teddy calling him again.

"I have a very special passenger." Teddy began. "It is Taylor Smith." Caputo recognized the name. "Taylor Smith the singer?"

"Yes. I understand she is worth a lot of money." Teddy's mind was working fast. "Probably someone could hold her for ransom for a lot of bucks." He was already thinking of an additional bonus. Teddy was hoping Caputo might be interested. "Hey…. That's a pretty good idea, Ted."

"Maybe you can give me a bonus?" Teddy knew that Caputo was impressed. "Yes, I think that could be arranged." Caputo agreed. He could see asking for at least a hundred thousand French Francs for her return. "I will meet you at the island with my gun crew." He hung up.

Teddy went back into the terminal. He met the five people and escorted them out to his plane. They followed, walking into the hot hanger.

Sylvia complained to him. "Twenty-five hundred francs is a lot of money for such a short trip."

"Look Lady, if you want to wait for the commercial commuter plane tomorrow, it will cost you a lot more than that," he bluffed.

Taylor's mom Sara said "It's ok Sylvia, as long as we get there on time. It will be an adventure." Taylor said nothing, hiding behind her dark sunglasses. She and Betty followed with Stanley who was struggling with the suitcases on the cart. When they saw the aircraft, Stanley exclaimed "We are flying in that old heap?"

"It is a fully certified aircraft, sonny. Just be glad I am allowing you to fly in it." Teddy growled.

"It's ok." Taylor's mother said. "This will be an adventure we can all talk about later."

Taylor was shocked. She was used to flying in luxury with the best aircraft. This thing didn't even look as if it could get off the ground. Teddy took the luggage cart from Stanley and told them to go ahead and board. He then stored the luggage in the storage compartment. *Four women really traveled with a lot of stuff,* he thought. He barely had enough room in the storage compartment. His shoulder began to hurt again but he ignored it. He needed another smoke badly.

As Stanley boarded the plane he saw Ron sitting near the front. "Who the hell are you? You will have to get off. We are a private charter."

"I have a ticket to ride" Ron objected. He wondered who this huge muscle bound creep was.

Sylvia added "We need to have the whole plane," she said stiffly, looking at Ron. "He is another passenger." Teddy called out from the doorway.

"He can't travel with us." Stanley replied. He opened his jacket showing a revolver in a holster on his belt.

"Look Sonny, I say who flies and who doesn't." Teddy replied. "Now find a seat and sit down. Or get off my plane."

"It's Ok, Stan. He looks ok." Taylor noted. The five newcomers moved to the front of the passenger compartment and found a seat. Ron moved to the very back row so they could all sit together.

Ron could not believe his eyes. He recognized Taylor Smith even though she was wearing dark sunglasses. He had seen some of her music videos and was impressed with her singing talent. While he was not a true fan, he had heard some of her songs and they were pretty good. He looked at the whole entourage. Taylor Smith was a blond haired knock-out beauty and was dressed in a pink and red outfit. The complaining woman, Sylvia was a brunette dressed in a conservative gray pantsuit with white sandals. The older, very attractive woman was also a blond and similarly dressed in tan pants and a red blouse and looked a lot like Taylor, so she must be her mother. Ron thought she looked like an older version of the actress in the movie pretty woman but with blond hair. The remaining woman was also a brunette and very pretty but younger and dressed in what appeared to be short sleeve yellow blouse and ragged jean shorts. All of the women except the mother who was wearing sneakers had sandals on, appropriate for summer wear. The ugly, muscle-bound bad-tempered strong man had a gray business suit and black tie and black loafers. As they were getting settled, the pilot closed up and sealed the back door hatch and moved up to the cockpit cabin. He stopped at a small refrigerator in a small galley near the front cockpit and took out some water bottles and distributed one to each passenger.

"Sorry, but we don't have a stewardess." Teddy noted. "This is about an hour long flight so make yourselves comfortable."

"Where is the co-pilot?" Ron asked from the rear of the plane. "And I thought it was about a 20-minute flight?"

"It's just me." Teddy turned and smiled at him with brown stained teeth. "And, yes, if you go by one of those commuter jets, it is about a 20 minute trip. This plane only travels about 150 miles an hour, not the 400 miles per hour of those commercial jobs." He turned and entered the cockpit. He was careful to draw the curtain closed behind him. He had brought a cooler with him that contained a six pack of beer.

Ron was somewhat disturbed by all that had happened. He was thinking that he had made a real bad decision to go on this charter. The pilot was an old pot-bellied scruffy looking guy. And now he was in a plane without a copilot and was considered an intruder by the celebrity party. Ron knew better than to ask Taylor for her autograph. He knew most celebrities preferred anonymity as much as possible. He was sorry for going on this charter; but now he was in it and he might as well sit back, make the best of it and take a nap. He hoped the trip in this old crate would be uneventful.

He figured once they were at Bora Bora he could put all of this behind him. Teddy sat in the cockpit and opened a can of beer from the cooler he had put under his seat. He was happy. He would make a pretty good profit today, and now a possible special bonus from Caputo.

Chapter 8
Day 1   3:45 PM

Teddy started the old aircraft and it slowly sputtered to life. He checked his fuel status. The tanks were a little over half full, and he had about a 400 mile range, so he should have enough fuel to get to Bora Bora and back. The weather report said there was a tropical storm headed this way around dusk. He should be safely back in Papeete by then, he thought. He then filed his flight plan with the airport control tower and requested permission to take off. The airport was not that busy so he received permission almost immediately. He had made this trip several hundred times so he knew it by heart. He would take off in a northwestern direction at a heading of 330 degrees, fly for 30 minutes and then change his heading to 275 degrees west. This would bring him within sight of either the islands of Bora Bora or Tupai. He knew that Caputo and his gang would be waiting at Tupai.

Teddy knew that the ransom would be pretty high to return an important celebrity singer like Taylor Smith to her freedom. He thought for a minute. What would Caputo do with the rest of his passengers? If Caputo let them live, they would implicate Teddy. Cooper Charters would be closed and he himself would be imprisoned for helping the kidnapers. He knew that Caputo would not want to disrupt the heroin delivery system since it was working so well. So, Caputo would probably take them with him and then kill them at sea after Teddy left for Bora Bora. If an investigation found that ll of these people were in his charter, it would not look good. He would have to fire Suzy Kwan and destroy any paperwork linking them to the charter. He wondered where he would find a better desk clerk. Wait a minute. He started thinking. If Caputo let the singer go after the ransom was paid, she would testify that Cooper was assisting Caputo. All this thinking made his head hurt. He would have to make up a story that his plane was having engine problems and that he had to divert to the Tupai Island for repairs.

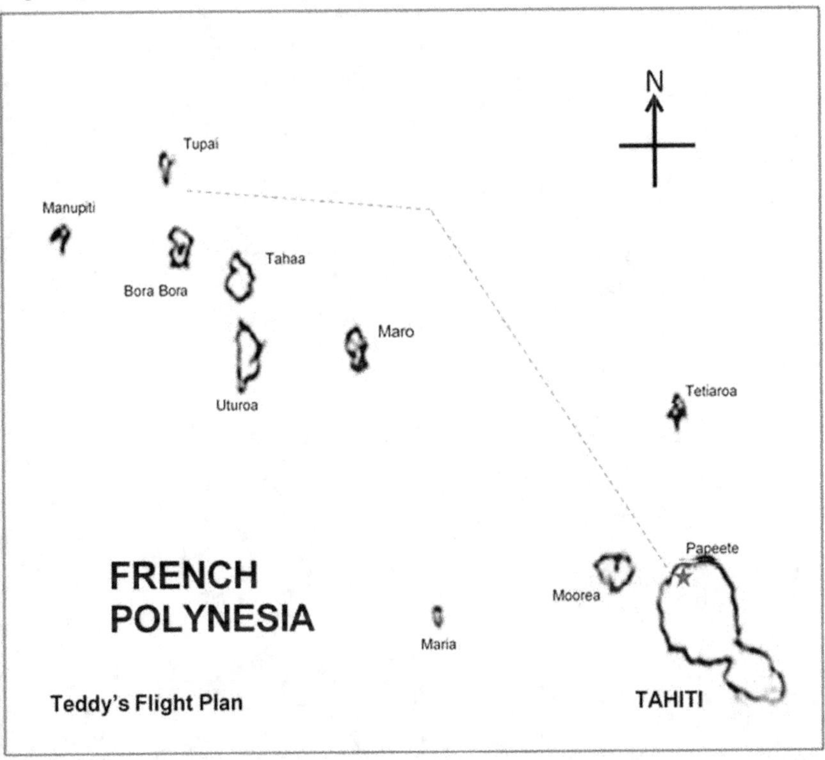

Caputo could rough him up a bit so that it looked like he wasn't involved. That way no one had to die. Caputo would have to make it look like his presence on Tupai was by pure chance. That could work. Caputo would grab the woman and take off, leaving the rest of the party behind. He could use the excuse to search their luggage to quietly take the drugs. It should work. He made the turn west and then put the plane on autopilot while he took out his satellite cell phone and texted Caputo his plan. He did not have a very good signal but hoped Caputo would catch on. His shoulder hurt now even worse. Damn, he thought. I got to have this looked at. He reached under his seat and pulled out another beer. He drank the beer and felt a little better. The phone beeped. Caputo had accepted his idea. He turned off the phone and hid it under the seat for now. He continued to drink the beer. The pain in his shoulder would not go away. Funny, He did not remember straining it.

CHAPTER 9
DAY 1   4:00 PM

Franklin Carrere paced across the arrival gate area at the Motu Muti Airport on Bora Bora. He was waiting for Taylor Smith's Gulfstream to land. It was already overdue by 30 minutes. He was the producer of the music video and photo shoot that was to be shot for Taylor. He was concerned about any delays in the shoot. He had arrived with his team of twenty people three days ago and scouted out several beaches for the video to be shot. The most promising beach was actually on another island, Tupai. It was perfect with its pristine sandy beaches, plenty of palm trees and no tourist sunbathers or swimmers. He had discussed moving the production to that island but was told by the Bora Bora Island environmental officials that such a large amount of people could badly affect the natural ecology of the island which was a sanctuary for exotic birds and sea turtles. He had approached the government bureau with an appeal and was waiting for their decision. He had included a small gift of cash to the responsible bureaucrats. Now Taylor was late. Every day delay would cost an extra $35,000 dollars. His team consisted of 20 cameramen, sound experts, music mixers, and technical support people. They all had to be fed, have nice hotel rooms and their normal salary. None of his people were complaining about being in Tahiti since Bora Bora was a nice place to work, but he was on a budget. Now that he was on Bora Bora he did not really like the foods they served, mostly dishes of raw fish and various fruits. He was a steak and potato person, and there was very little of this in Tahiti.

His phone rang. He grabbed it. It was Sylvia, Taylor's agent.

"Frank," she started, "We are at Papeete but have run into a little bit of a delay.

The Gulfstream charter aircraft is down for maintenance."

"Oh no….what are you going to do?" Franklin exclaimed.

"Oh, don't worry. We're flying over on an island charter aircraft. We'll get there but probably a little later than expected." Sylvia explained.

"Ok." Franklin was relieved. "We want to start shooting tomorrow morning if possible. I found a nice beach that sort of fits her description."

"I doubt if Taylor will want to do it tomorrow. We all have a bad case of jet lag." "Ok. But know that every extra day will cost her."

"Stop worrying. We will be there in about an hour…we can discuss it then." She hung up. The old seaplane was taxiing out to the runway. Sylvia had planned this photo shoot and now there was this problem with the fancy jet charter and she and Taylor were forced to fly on this rattletrap of a plane. She had argued with Taylor about doing the video in San Diego where there was a perfect beach for the photo shoot, but Taylor had insisted on this trip and Taylor always got her way. Since Sylvia was Taylor's agent, she always got a percentage of what Taylor made, and it had been a very prosperous deal for her, even if Taylor was somewhat stubborn and spoiled. She just hoped this all worked out. The release of the new album was supposed to be timed with the release of the music video to get the most market saturation. Not that Taylor had anything to worry about. Her fans would immediately go out and buy her album. She had sold over 10 million copies of the last album and her fans were clamoring for more. Sylvia resigned herself to flying in this wreck of an airplane and just hoped they would get to Bora Bora intact. She settled down in the seat, trying to get comfortable.

Across the aisle sat Betty, Taylor's best friend, frustrated at the delay to get to the video shoot. She had been with Taylor since grade school and often helped Taylor to write her songs. Taylor was the singer and boss but often used Betty as a sounding board for issues that came up. They were a team and were inseparable. Now they were traveling in this bad-smelling rattletrap of a plane and she was not happy. She tried to use her cell phone in the airport but her battery was low and there were no charging ports in this old aircraft. How was she going to update her internet commitments? She was Taylor's official access to her fan base and Face Book pages.

Chapter 10
Day 1   4:10 PM

Snake Caputo was on his 56-foot yacht. The yacht was a gift from one of his customers who owed him a lot of money. The name on the boat was '*PIRATE*' which was very appropriate for his line of work. His real name was 'Jose' Caputo but he had his minions call him 'Snake.' That sounded a lot meaner and more dangerous, he thought. He had grown up on the islands and had struggled to become the top crime lord by violently eliminating any competition. His competitors were often abducted and lost at sea, usually with a cement block wired to their feet. He controlled all of the prostitution, loan sharking, drugs and protection on most of the islands except Bora Bora which was a separate tourist vacation paradise. The officials on Bora Bora paid him well to stay away from the tourist trade. He did not mind as long as they paid. He had his typical crew of a boat captain and four of his gunmen with him on the boat. He had received Teddy's text message and it made sense. They would wait for him to land and then move in and act like pirates. They would snatch the girl and search through the luggage compartment and retrieve the concealed drugs. They would have to rough up Teddy a bit so that his other passengers would not suspect his involvement. Teddy knew he would get a big bonus so he would be ok with it. He checked on the internet for Taylor Smith and she was supposedly worth several million dollars. So now he figured maybe to ask for half a million dollars to return her. She would have a bodyguard with her so he might have to be eliminated. For that much cash he was willing to take that chance. His boat was already just about a half mile out from Tupai Island. They were lucky; there were no scheduled tourist visits to the uninhabited protected island today. His main man, Arno Tuvala, was already scanning the eastern sky with binoculars for Teddy's aircraft.

"He should be coming by now." Arno said.

"Have patience. He will be here," Caputo answered. Caputo knew that Teddy was scared shitless of him, with good reason. The previous charter aircraft owner had disappeared without a trace, plane and all. That pilot had tried to double cross Caputo. Caputo had pictures of the tortured pilot and had shown them to Teddy to get him to take over the delivery process for the drugs. Now Teddy would do anything he asked. Once they had the celebrity singer they would cruise over to Maria Island and stow her over there. That island was uninhabited but had some old wood buildings that were used by whaling crews back in the 1800's. He had used the whaling station before and it was well suited for his purposes. He had adequate supplies stored there to wait a week or two until he got the ransom. He had not decided yet if he would kill the singer or let her go once he was paid off. There would be quite a bit of turmoil over her disappearance and he might have to hide out in Indonesia for a year or two.

"I think I see a plane" Arno said.

"Good. Let's get prepared." Caputo replied. His men got their weapons out and loaded them. The three other gunmen were Chino, Uri and Huwala. They all had Uzis, a compact automatic 9mm machine gun with magazines containing 30 rounds. Arno and Caputo both carried Glock 17s, semi-automatic 9mm pistols. Caputo doubted that he would get any resistance from the bodyguard when facing these heavily armed men but told them to be prepared anyway. If they had to shoot the body guard he was ok with that.

CHAPTER 11
DAY 1   4:15 PM

Taylor Smith was very tired. She had been travelling from New York for over 16 hours in the Gulfstream aircraft with only stops to re-fuel at San Diego and Hawaii. Now she was in this rattletrap aircraft with no luxury amenities. Although the seat was uncomfortable, she would try to make the best of it. Her mother had said that this would be an adventure. Her mother was always looking at the good side of things. Taylor was not feeling that it was a good adventure but would try to endure it. They would be in Bora Bora in an hour. She figured she might as well take a nap. The droning of the propeller engines was putting everyone else to sleep. She could look out the window but all she could see was endless blue water. She started to think about the music video and the song she had selected for the video shoot. She hoped that the production company had found a beach close to her specifications. She had already decided which bathing suit she would wear. It was a sexy number, but that is what sold these days. She was still thinking of this when she nodded off to sleep.

The bodyguard Stanley did not like this aircraft or the pilot. But since everyone else went along with it, he would, too. Since Taylor said it was alright, he could not really argue against it. He also did not like the close proximity of the strange guy sitting in the back. They should have kicked him off before taking off. But the man was older, appeared to be harmless and stayed to himself. Stan was already daydreaming, thinking of spending some time on the Bora Bora beaches and doing some heavy partying with some of the local ladies while Taylor was doing the video shoot. He noticed that everyone else was sleeping so he figured it was ok to take a nap also.

Ron Pritchard tried to read his book but the droning of the engines was getting to him also. He put the book down and leaned against the window and fell asleep.

Teddy had made the turn west and set the autopilot on. The pain in his shoulder was getting worse. He reached under his seat and pulled out another beer. It wasn't very cold but he popped the cap and chugged it down. It helped the pain he thought. He began to look for the island of Tupai.

Teddy hoped Caputo would follow his proposed plan. If Caputo had to kill the passengers, he might want to eliminate any witnesses like Teddy. That was not a pleasant thought. He put the thought out of his mind. If he got an additional 5000 franc bonus for delivering the singer, he could take a small vacation on the beach with a couple of friendly ladies he knew. Now that was a pleasant thought. He checked his fuel gages. They were now below half but he still had enough to get to Bora Bora with fuel to spare. He could top off the tanks before the return trip to Papeete. The engines were running normal as was typical. The old plane was rugged and durable. He would have to trim the fuel control and throttle a bit on one engine to make it sound as if there was a problem. He looked ahead. He should be getting close to Tupai soon. The pain returned. Jesus, he thought, it was getting worse. He really wanted another cigarette but it would have to wait until he landed at Tupai.

CHAPTER 12
DAY 1   4:35 PM

Arno saw the plane first. "I see it. It's coming this way," he exclaimed. They turned the boat towards the island and sped up.

Caputo now saw the aircraft. It was Teddy's amphibian all right. It was at about 5000 feet altitude. But he wasn't coming any lower. It looked as though Teddy was going to bypass the eastern side of the island and land toward the western side. Why was he doing that? It would take them longer to approach the aircraft if he landed way over there. But the G73 Mallard kept going, not even turning toward the island. "What the heck?" he said out loud.

Arno pointed at the plane. "He's not turning," he exclaimed. "I can see that!" Caputo noted. "What the hell is he doing?' They watched as the plane droned out of sight.

"Should we follow it?" Randy, the boat captain asked.

"We don't know where he is going." Caputo replied. He ran to the bridge and took out a map chart. The only other island in that direction was Manupiti. Why would he go there? "Get on the radio and see if you can contact him. Then set course for Manupiti." They tried radioing Teddy repeatedly but got no response. It was very frustrating to be so close to the rich prize and then watch it fly away. He would have words with Teddy over this. Maybe he had a good reason to miss the rendezvous. Caputo scanned the sea around the island. Was there a Coast Guard ship nearby? He could not see anything. Very puzzling, he thought.

Manupiti was a large island atoll with a population of about 1200 people. It was a tourist island known for its beautiful mountain scenery and picturesque skin-diving lagoon. Why would Teddy head in that direction?

Caputo checked his satellite phone for any new text messages. There were none. He was starting to get angry. He tried to call Teddy on the satellite phone but got no answer. What the heck was going on? He wondered.

CHAPTER 13
DAY 1   6:45 PM

Ron Prichard woke up from his nap. He looked out the window. They were still flying over a vast expanse of blue water. They should be getting pretty close to Bora Bora by now. He looked at his watch. "Jesus!" he exclaimed. It had been three hours since they left Papeete. What the heck was going on? He got out of his seat and moved toward the front of the cabin. Every one of the other passengers was asleep. He moved to where Stanley was sitting and shook his shoulder.

Stanley woke with a start. "What…" He managed to exclaim as he turned to look at Ron. "What the hell do you want?" he sneered.

"Look at the time." Ron whispered. "We should have gotten to Bora Bora by now.

What's going on?"

Stan looked at his watch. "Oh my god; what the hell is going on?"

"What's the matter?" Taylor said groggily as she woke up and looked at the two men.

"I don't know, but I am going to find out." Stanley said as he got out of his seat and moved toward the cockpit. Ron followed him.

As they pushed the curtain aside, they found Teddy leaning to his left, his head down, in the pilot seat.

"Did he fall asleep?" Stan said as he shook Teddy's shoulder. "Hey, wake up," he shouted. There was No response from Teddy.

Ron pushed Stanley aside and put his hand on Teddy's neck. "He has no pulse. I think he's dead," Ron said calmly.

"What the hell?" Stanley said. "What the hell are we going to do now? Who is going to fly the damned plane?"

"Are you a pilot?" Ron asked him. Stan replied "No……are you?"

"I have had a couple of lessons in a Cessna but I'm not really qualified to fly a multi-engine aircraft." Ron replied calmly. "How about one of the women?" he asked.

"I don't think so. But we can ask." Stan turned and went back to the passenger cabin. By now everyone was awake and the women were busy chatting among themselves.

"Can any of you fly a plane? The pilot is dead." Stanley said. Tact was not one of Stan's better qualities. The women began to get hysterical and started screaming.

Ron pushed by him. "Settle down," he said firmly but quietly. "Answer the question." The women looked at each other and all shook their heads no.

Ron looked at Taylor. "Ok. I have had a few lessons but I am not familiar with this aircraft, so bear with me."

"Are you sure you can fly this thing?" Taylor asked. She was getting scared. "Like I said, I have had a couple of lessons in a Cessna. I will give it a try unless you have another option." Ron was still talking calmly.

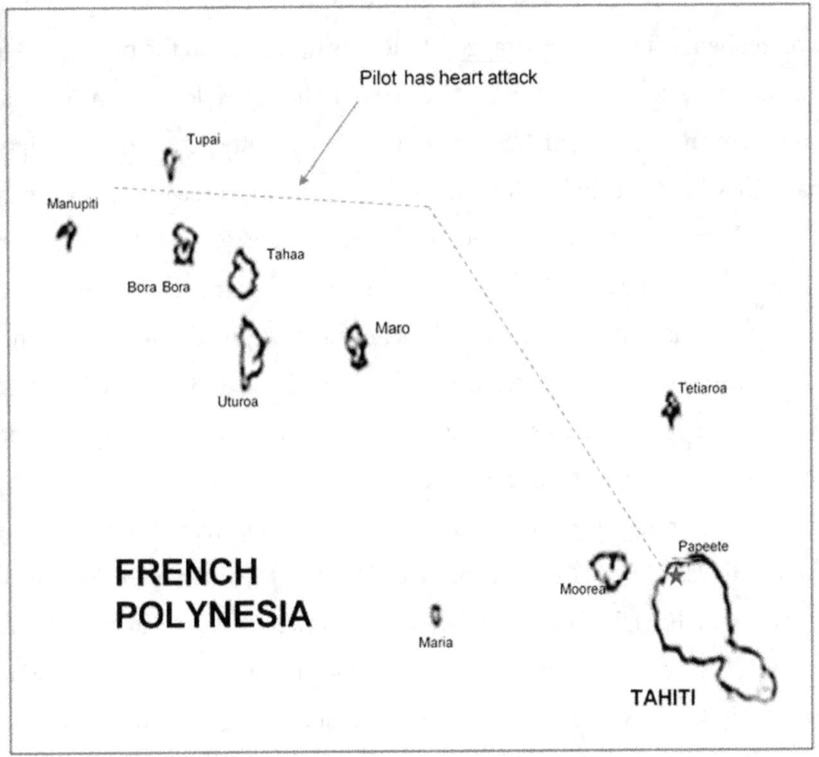

"No….it looks like you are it." Taylor said, smiling at him. Maybe he could fly it.

Ron turned to them.

"Ok. If I were you, I would take out the life vests and get familiar with them." Ron pointed to the life vests under the seats. "This thing supposedly can land in the water but I didn't get to any lessons on landings yet." Ron smiled back. He wondered if he really could fly this old crate.

"Oh my God…We are going to die." Sylvia muttered. "Be quiet Silvia." Taylor hissed at her.

"Ok. Just be calm and I will try to get us down somewhere safe." Ron turned back to the cockpit. Stanley followed him.

"What should we do with him?" Stanley pointed at the dead pilot.

"Put him in one of the last seats, as far away from the women as possible." Ron replied. After Stanley dragged Teddy away, Ron sat in the pilot seat. He looked at the controls and gages. He saw that the auto pilot was on and that they were on a heading of 275 degrees west. Apparently they had flown right past Bora Bora. He looked for a map chart but did not see one. Apparently Teddy did not keep charts or records in the cockpit. Ron knew this was in violation of FAA rules. His flight instructor had always emphasized having the correct charts and flight manuals before allowing anyone to fly his plane.

I wonder where the heck we are, he thought. He asked Stanley to bring up his carry-on bag from his seat. Stan did this and then sat in the co-pilot seat. Ron looked through the bag and pulled out the tourist map he had. If the pilot had steered directly toward Bora Bora, they must have passed near the control tower at Moto Muti airport. He picked up the radio mike. He hoped it was set to the right frequency. "Moto Muti tower, do you read me?" There was only static. If they were so far away that the tower did not read them, God only knew where they were. If the airspeed was 150 miles per hour they would have traveled almost 400 miles from Papeete.

He scanned the fuel gages. They were almost on empty. *My God, what are we going to do?* Ron thought to himself. He was starting to sweat heavily. He reached over to the aircraft transponder and changed the setting from 2000 to 7700 (a Mayday signal). He scanned the horizon in all directions and did not see anything. If any aircraft or airports were in the area they would recognize the transponder signal as a mayday. There were some dark clouds with lightening on the horizon. It looked as if a storm was headed their way. Ron wondered even if he was able to land this plane on the water, would it survive a tropical storm? He figured their chances were better to land near an island, any island. He turned on the radio again. "Mayday, Mayday, Mayday. This is the Cooper Charter out of Papeete; our pilot is dead and we are out of fuel and about to crash."

Stanley looked at him. Crash? That did not sound good. He hoped this guy knew what he was doing.

Chapter 14
Day 1   6:50 PM

Franklin Carrere used one of the white curtesy phones to talk to airport information. He told the operator that he needed to talk to someone about an overdue plane. She transferred him to one of the people at the airport information desk.

"I want to report an overdue flight." Franklin stated seriously. "They left Papeete over three hours ago to land here and have not arrived yet."

"What airline was that?" the woman on the other line asked. At least she was speaking English.

"I believe they said it was a charter aircraft out of Papeete," he replied excitedly. "They said they would be here hours ago."

"The only charter due from Papeete is Cooper's. Is that the flight?" she asked calmly.

"Yes, I guess that was the one. Some very important people were on that flight." "Well, I am familiar with that charter. He sometimes stops at Tupai to show them the natural beauty of that island. It is against the rules but he does it anyway," she explained.

"Well, they aren't answering my phone call to them." He was getting irritated.

"I don't think there are any cell towers at that island, sir. You need a satellite phone or a radio to communicate with them if that is where they are," she replied calmly.

"I am worried that they may have crashed in the sea," he exclaimed.

"That is very unlikely. They would have sent a Mayday signal to the tower. Anyway, that charter is an amphibian and can land in the water on floats." "Well….can't you do something?" He was getting really angry now.

"I can check with the tower sir. What is your name and number so that I can get back to you?"

Franklin gave her his name and cell phone number and then hung up. He was very frustrated and he doubted if she was going to do anything. He walked back to the arrival gate area. He began to go over the cost of delaying the video shoot in his mind. Taylor would have to pay a big bonus over the agreed contract if she wanted him to stay additional days. *Damn that Woman.* He thought to himself. They could have already shot the music video on a beach in San Diego and he would be home with his family.

The control tower at Motu Muti had heard the faint mayday and tried to radio back. The controller had wondered earlier why the charter aircraft had flown past without landing. He had attempted to radio the pilot but had gotten no answer. *This was very strange,* he thought. He alerted his supervisor that he had received a Mayday signal from the charter aircraft. Their limited radar had shown the aircraft actually passing Bora Bora and then vanishing as it went out of radar range. When the information operator called to ask about the charter the flight controller replied that the plane had sent out a Mayday signal and might have to do a water landing. The information woman called Franklin back.

"Sir, it appears there is some trouble with the charter flight." She tried to be calm. "Well, what is it?" Franklin demanded.

"Apparently they sent out a Mayday signal." She did not like his tone

"Just what the hell does that mean?" He asked.

"They may have to make an emergency landing." She tried to explain

"Oh God." This can't be happening he thought.

"That is all I can tell you." She hung up.

"Jesus." Franklin staggered over to a chair and sat down. What was he going to do now? He wondered. His company had invested a significant amount of funding to do the music video. Since it was for Taylor Smith, they would receive a lot of exposure and publicity when they released the video which should result in more business.

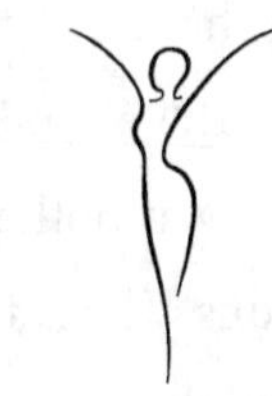

CHAPTER 15
DAY 1   6:55 PM

Ron Pritchard was getting worried. He had no idea where they were and the aircraft was almost out of fuel. He saw that they were flying on a heading of 275 degrees and figured that would have put them directly in line with Bora Bora. He decided to try the radio again.

"Mayday, Mayday, Mayday. To anyone hearing this, we are about to land in the water. Our pilot is dead and we are out of fuel. We are on a course heading 275 degrees out of Bora Bora. I repeat, Mayday, Mayday, Mayday." Ron talked into the mike.

"What does Mayday mean?" Stanley asked. He was getting very nervous and concerned about the thought of a water landing out in the middle of the ocean.

"It is like an SOS but more typical for aircraft use." Ron was too busy to explain further. He studied the switches and gages. They were cruising at about only 5000 feet altitude, probably since the cabin of the aircraft was not pressurized and there were no oxygen masks in the cabin or cockpit. They did not have enough fuel to turn around and try to go back. He had to find someplace to land. He located the auto pilot switch but did not switch it off yet. He had no experience with a multi-engine aircraft. There were duplicate controls for the engines. He knew how to steer the plane and use the rudder to turn the aircraft and flaps to climb or descend but each aircraft had specific landing characteristics. And there was no manual in the cockpit that he could find. The old pilot must have flown this crate for so many years that he didn't even bother to use a manual. That was also totally against FAA regulations. The starboard engine was beginning to cough, low on fuel. He trimmed the fuel control back to neutral on that engine and it smoothed out. The aircraft tilted to starboard slightly and the autopilot triggered a warning bell. He turned off the autopilot and used the rudder to stabilize the plane but it was now pushing him off the 275 degree heading. Then the starboard engine just died. How long could he hold altitude with only one engine? The altimeter showed that they were now at about 4500 feet but were slowly losing altitude, probably due to only one engine operating. He could adjust the fuel supply to the port engine to increase thrust and regain altitude, but that fuel gage was near empty also. Stanley watched him intently. So far Ron appeared to know what he was doing but Stan was still worried. He began to sweat profusely.

"Is there anything I can do to help?" He asked nervously.

"Yeah, start looking for land, any land." Ron was still working the controls. Ron was not comfortable about a water landing. He supposed that he could slowly lower altitude and cut back the engine power and lower the flaps like in a Cessna, but he was not familiar with these controls at all. He looked for the lever to adjust the flaps and thought he recognized it. Maybe he could land it in the water, but what then? If they were near land he could taxi over to an island and beach it on the shore. Hopefully the natives on these islands were friendly. The sky was getting darker and it began to rain. *This is just great*, Ron thought. What else could go wrong?

CHAPTER 16
DAY 1   6:56 PM

Snake Caputo was confused. Teddy had arranged the rendezvous and then had flown right by. Why would he do that?

"I just heard a Mayday on the radio!" the boat captain, Randy shouted at him. "What was it?" Caputo responded?

"It was very faint, but something about the pilot of a charter airplane being dead." The captain exclaimed.

"Jesus." Caputo muttered. The damn Teddy guy must have died. That was why they flew past the island. He must have had the aircraft on auto pilot. He had wondered about Teddy when he first hired him. The man was in terrible shape, but he had always been dependable . . . until today. Maybe all they had to do was follow the flight path and "rescue"' the occupants.

"How much fuel do we have?" Caputo asked.

"We could go about a hundred miles or so, if we cruise slowly." The captain

noted.

"That won't do. Let's make for Maupiti and refuel. Then we will go looking for an airplane." Caputo replied. At least it was an amphibian. Once it ran out of fuel, it would be on the surface of the ocean, he hoped. Maybe they had already diverted to Maupiti if someone on board knew how to fly an airplane. Randy reminded him that there was a tropical storm warning for this evening.

"Great. That's all we need." Caputo replied.

"Arno. Call up our contacts on Maupiti and have them check any incoming flights to see if Teddy's airplane landed there." Caputo commanded. He might still be able to recover their cargo and snatch the girl singer. What had started out to be a very profitable venture was now turning out very bad. Now he had lost Teddy and the potential celebrity ransom. Also, his drug shipment was probably at the bottom of the ocean. He groaned. He had a meager supply in reserve but not enough to supply his clients until the next shipment. His clients could start looking for an alternate supplier. He did not need any competition right now.

CHAPTER 17
DAY 1   6:58 PM

The tower flight control operator on Bora Bora kept trying to radio the charter aircraft. The plane was out of radar range so he did not have a position for it. He had wondered why the Cooper Charter had flown out of his control area instead of landing as expected. If the pilot was dead, why didn't the co-pilot answer? His supervisor put out an alert for the Coast Guard and then called the local FAA representative at Papeete. There was a definite chance the plane was already down somewhere on the ocean.

Captain Patrice Bourne on the French Coast Guard cutter 'Renégat' ordered his crew to quarters. Captain Bourne thought of himself as a sophisticated French gentleman who lived for the better things in life. He had received his commission by political favors to his family. He was an easy going commander so his crew did not mind his aloofness. His ship was currently at dockside in Papeete when they received word of the Mayday from the flight control operator on Bora Bora. His ship was a small craft as coast guard vessels go, only 45 feet long with a crew of ten. It was an old French patrol craft basically used to rescue boaters who had hit reefs or search for swimmers that were reported missing. Since it was such a small ship, it did not have a helicopter, which would have helped in finding a downed aircraft. They would have to try anyway. He looked at the charts and noted that the missing plane's flight plan was from Papeete to Bora

Bora. So, he would head for Bora and then proceed west from there. If they were indeed on a course heading that was 275 degrees west, he might get lucky. The message he received was that the pilot had died, so the aircraft probably crashed into the sea. If this was the case, they might only find some debris, since sharks were usually around to eliminate any survivors from a crash. The weather report did not look good either. A storm was coming in from the west. They would probably just make it to Bora Bora before they had to put into the port to avoid the storm. He called the French consulate and informed them that a rescue operation was in progress and any help from the French military would be appreciated. He knew that a French military plane was visiting the island and it could help in the search. If the small seaplane was caught in the storm it could be forced down. He hoped that was not the case.

CHAPTER 18
DAY 1   7:30 PM

Ron was getting desperate. He had tried the radio again but doubted that the tower at Bora Bora heard him due to the distance. His airspeed showed that he was around 120 knots. He did some calculating in his head. That would be equivalent to around 100 miles an hour. By his watch they had left Papeete a little over three hours ago. It was starting to get dark and it was starting to rain. Three hours flying would put them over 350 miles from Papeete, or almost 200 miles past Bora Bora. His tourist map did not show anything that far west. Granted, they had slowed quite a bit when the one engine died, but that still put them in an area of the Pacific where there were no islands, he thought. The right engine had died a half hour ago, totally out of fuel. The fuel gage for the left engine was now on zero. They had lost altitude to about 1000 feet. They would have to land pretty soon. They had drifted off the original course and were heading slightly north but Ron was not watching the compass heading but instead was looking for land. He saw lightening in the distance and it started to rain harder. Ron thought Great, as if everything else isn't bad enough; we are riding right into a tropical storm.

"Look over there!" Stanley pointed off to the right. In the twilight gloom there was a spot of land.

"We'll never make it." Ron said calmly as he turned the aircraft toward what looked like a small island. They were still losing altitude, and the left engine was now sputtering due to running out of fuel.

"I can see it." Stanley said. It was actually a lot closer than Ron thought. It must be a very small island. As they got closer it looked like a small atoll. There was a ring of land with a center lagoon. One could see that waves were breaking on what looked like a ring of reefs around the atoll. If they could land in the lagoon, they would be ok, he thought. As it was, the aircraft was not going to get that far. The left engine died all together. They were now coasting but were too low to get to the inner lagoon.

Ron had an idea. If he put the nose down to gain speed he could pull up near the water with the full flaps and maybe gain enough altitude to maybe make it into the lagoon. He turned to Stanley.

"Grab the co-pilot control wheel. When I tell you, we both need to pull back as hard as we can."

"Ok." Stanley was not really hearing Ron. He grabbed the control wheel but He was terrified that they were going to crash.

Ron put the plane into a dive.

"What are you doing?" Stanley screamed. "Get ready." Ron said.

"No . . ." Stanley pulled back on the control too soon, before Ron was ready. And the plane started to side slip and stall. Ron tried to correct with the rudder and pulled back on the control, but they were now very close to the reef around the island. They weren't going to make it.

Ron finally got it straightened out but they hit the reef at a shallow angle. The right side float hit first and then the main fuselage hit. The plane bounced upward from the impact and floated over the narrow beach and into the water in the lagoon. The plane coasted a bit and then stopped. There was a lot of screaming from the passenger cabin.

"Why did you do that?" Ron asked Stanley, angry. Stanley wasn't answering him. The impact with the reef had thrown him against the control panel and he was unconscious. Ron looked at him and saw that Stan's head was bleeding badly.

"Well . . . any landing without blowing up is a good one, I guess." Ron said to himself. They had at least made it into the lagoon but he feared the plane was damaged. He got out of the pilot's seat and went into the main cabin. The screaming had stopped at least.

"Is everyone ok back here?" He asked. The aircraft was silent except for the rain pattering on the roof.

"Did we land?" Taylor asked him.

"Sort of . . . We hit the reef but we are down in one piece." Ron said. He looked around. One of the women obviously had a broken arm and was in pain. It was Sylvia, Taylor's agent. The others all looked pretty good, but Betty was going to have a large bruise on her forehead. Taylor and her mother appeared to be ok.

"Where are we?" Taylor asked. "Where is Stan?" she asked.

"I don't really know where we are, but we are in the lagoon of a small island atoll. Maybe there are people here that can radio for help." Ron was trying to be a calming, positive influence for the ladies. "Stan hit his head on landing and is knocked out."

Taylor rushed into the cockpit and tried to wake Stanley. "Will he be ok?" she asked Ron.

"I don't know." Ron replied. "We will have to wait and see when he wakes up." Ron noticed that the plane had a slight list to starboard. *Probably damaged the starboard float when we hit the reef,* he thought. He followed Taylor into the main cabin. He noticed that there was some water on the floor. It appeared to be getting deeper. Oh no....The fuselage must have been damaged or holed on impact, breaking the water tight integrity of the fuselage body.

"Look. Can you guys' swim to the shore? We appear to be sinking," he stated as calmly as he could. This started some screaming again, mostly from Betty and Silvia.

"Calm down. It's not that far, but put on the life preservers." He walked to the back and opened the entrance hatch. Thank God it had not jammed shut. He looked outside. The plane had drifted in a circle so that the front of the plane was now pointing the way they had come in. The tip of the right wing was sinking low and was almost in the water, but the left float was still holding the plane up. The impact must have ripped off the right float, he thought. Although it was twilight, they could see a small island about 90 yards away. It was raining harder now and the wind was blowing hard. He helped the girls put on the life vests which appeared to be functional. Then he helped them to the entry hatch and into the water. It was getting darker. He told them to swim to the island while they could still see it. Silvia couldn't swim but Taylor grabbed her life vest and sort of towed her. He wondered what to do with Stanley? He moved back up to the cockpit, and dragged Stan into the main cabin. He saw a flashlight near the old refrigerator and grabbed it and shoved it into his pants. Then he saw a package containing an inflatable life raft beside the refrigerator. He hadn't noticed that before. The inside lights in the cabin went out as the influx of water shorted out the electrical fuse box. There was only one life preserver left and he put it on Stan. He had to inflate it with his breath since the pull tab did not work to inflate it. He took off his shoes and tied them together so that they were around his neck. Ron took the life raft over to the hatch and opened the air tank to inflate the life raft. Nothing happened. The tank valve had rusted and the compressed air had leaked out over time. "Wonderful," he said in disgust. He threw the life raft into the water. It floated toward the island. He pushed Stanley into the water and then got out himself. He grabbed Stan's life preserver and started to swim for the shore. It was almost dark now. The island was just a lighter grey blob of color compared to the darkness of the water. It was difficult swimming with the dead weight of Stanley. The wind and rain had increased, making it even more difficult to swim. He had gotten to about 40 yards from shore when there was a tug on the life vest. Was Stanley coming to? He turned in the water and saw a fin move past him. Sharks! And Stanley had been bleeding. One of them came close to him and he kicked it as hard as he could and started to swim faster toward shore. There was another tug on the life vest and he heard Stan grunt. He turned again. There was a dark stain in the water and it could only be blood. He kicked out at another shark although he could sense it more than see it. He swam harder again. His foot finally touched the sandy bottom and he struggled up to the shore. He dragged Stanley up on to the beach. The yellow life raft had also washed up on shore. He took out the flashlight and shined it on Stan. His right leg was gone below the knee and he was bleeding profusely. He took Stan's belt off and tied it as a tourniquet above the knee where the leg had been severed.

The women saw the light and walked over to him. When they saw all the blood they started to scream again. The rain was really starting to pound them now. He dragged Stan over to the palm trees and told the women to follow. He then turned around and headed to the beach. The lightning lit up the beach where he had seen the life raft. He grabbed the life raft and headed back to the small cluster of survivors. Ron found a couple pieces of drift wood and arranged the life raft in the palm trees into sort of a lean- to with the back of it toward the wind-driven rain. Everyone was already soaked to the skin but it was still better just to get out of the rain. The women all huddled together. He told the girls to get under the raft. He moved Stan under the raft and used the flashlight to check on Stanley. He was still breathing. The makeshift tourniquet had slowed the blood but it was still bleeding. He tried to tighten the belt but ran out of punched holes. He looked around for a stick and found a small piece of driftwood, so he used it to tighten the belt by twisting it and prying one end under the belt. That helped stopping the bleeding but Stan had already lost an awful lot of blood.

"Will he live?" Taylor asked him as the women huddled together under the life raft, out of the rain for the moment.

"He's lost a lot of blood. We need to get him hospitalized as soon as possible." Ron replied. The wind was howling. He tied some of the straps attached to the life raft to the nearby palm trees and a piece of driftwood he had pushed into the sand about a foot and hoped it would hold.

"Are there any people on this island?" She asked.

"I don't know." Ron said. "It is a very small atoll; I didn't see any buildings from the air."

"Are you going out to look?" Taylor asked.

"Yeah, I guess I should." Ron said, resigned to being wet. He instructed the women to try to stay under the raft and hold on to the raft tie straps so it wouldn't blow away. He gave the flash light to Taylor but told her to conserve the battery. He slipped on his shoes and crawled out of the makeshift tent. It was dark and rainy. He could not see very well in the little light left. He turned toward the small hill behind him with more palm trees and underbrush and staggered upward toward them. He climbed the hill and looked for any signs of civilization. There were no huts or any lights except the occasional lightening burst. He could see a couple of other small islands on the atoll when the lightening flashed, but no buildings, just groups of palm trees and brush. He returned to the small tent and entered.

"There are no people here as far as I can tell," he told Taylor. "What will we do?" She asked.

"The aircraft transponder will send out a signal and should be picked up by any search plane or boat." Ron reassured her. "For now, let's just ride out the storm."

Taylor was miserable. It was getting cooler and she was wet, cold and tired. She huddled together with the other girls for warmth and thought, *My God, how could have this happened?* She fell into an uncomfortable sleep. The other girls huddled up to her. Sylvia was in great pain and was crying. Taylor's Mom, Sara, tried to hold on to both Taylor and the raft. The wind was blowing hard but the raft stayed in place. Taylor's girlfriend, Betty, tried to comfort Sylvia but was not having much success.

Ron stayed on the other side of the raft with Stan between him and the women. He hoped he was right about the transponder. He knew that the transponder batteries were only good for a few days. Since he was with an important celebrity like Taylor, he figured that the whole world would soon be looking for her. He felt that they would be rescued very soon. At least he hoped so. Although he was wet and cold, he did finally fall into a troubled sleep from all of the terror of trying to land the unfamiliar plane and sheer exhaustion.

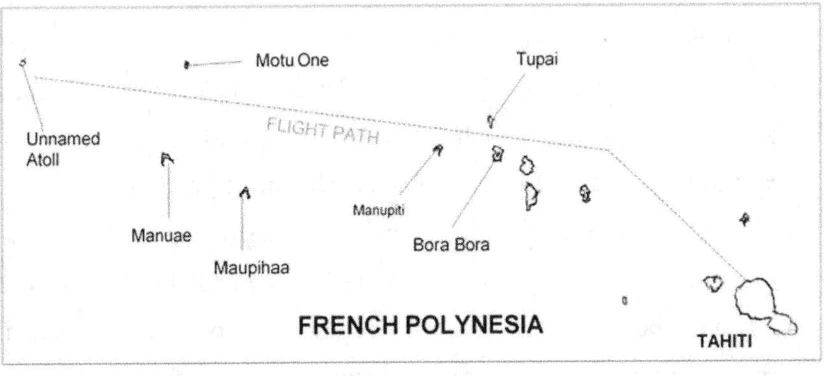

Ron crash lands on the unnamed atoll.

Chapter 19
Day 1   8:45 PM

Franklin Carrere was now fully terrified and disgusted. The news he had heard was that Taylor's charter aircraft was lost and probably down at sea. He really needed this contract. If Taylor's party was down with no survivors, he was going to have to pack up and head home, all at his own cost. Why hadn't Taylor been satisfied with using the beach outside of San Diego? It didn't make any sense. His instinct told him that he should stay and wait for them to be rescued. But the cost was killing him. He had called the French authorities several times and asked about the search. They had only replied that everything that could be done was being done. The search could not proceed due to the tropical storm coming in. Taylor's charter plane was now 4 hours overdue and it was getting dark outside. He called his friends in California and told them that Taylor Smith's plane had crashed at sea and her survival was doubtful. In minutes this message was out on the internet and thousands of Taylor's rabid fans became hysterical.

The French Military plane had taken off and was searching for the downed plane or any wreckage. Chances were since it was an amphibian aircraft it would simply be out of fuel and bobbing along on the sea. The problem was that the tropical storm front was coming in fast from the west and that would hamper any rescue operations. As the storm hit, the search plane had to reverse course and return to Bora Bora. The French authorities realized that the charter aircraft, if it had landed on the sea, would now drift with wind from the storm, causing the search pattern to expand. They should, however, be able to home in on the transponder signal from the plane which would make it easier. They figured they would have better success in the morning after the storm passed. If the survivors stayed on the plane, they probably would be ok as long as the plane did not sink.

The French patrol boat had to put into Bora Bora for the night. Captain Bourne was aware that if there were any survivors from a crashed airplane they would be difficult to spot at night in the storm. Using his typical French logic, the captain would get his boat ready to set out again at first light after the storm had passed to resume the search. He figured he would go ashore and eat a good meal in one of the fancy tourist restaurants.

CHAPTER 20
DAY 1   10:00 PM

The word of the disappearance of Taylor Smith had spread fast on the internet and her fan base began to pester the US coast guard and Navy, asking if they were planning to join the search. A Navy missile cruiser, the USS Preble, out of Pearl Harbor in Hawaii was on a training patrol close to Tahiti and was contacted by the Pacific Fleet Admiral at Pearl to head to Papeete to join in the search. This ship was an Aegis Navy Cruiser of 9800 tons with two SH-60B helicopters and a crew of 330 people. The ship's captain was Gerome Anderson and he did not particularly approve of this assignment. It was poor use of a Ticonderoga Class Aegis Class vessel with enough armament that could have taken out half of the Japanese fleet if it had been available in World War II. But he had to follow orders so he would make this the best search and rescue effort that the Navy could perform. He gave orders to head for the harbor at Papeete. They would wait out the storm in port and head out in the morning. He contacted the US Embassy on Papeete and informed them of the situation and that his ship had been assigned to the search and rescue of the small charter aircraft.

Captain Anderson was in his forties, an Annapolis graduate who had selected the US Navy as his career. He was a proficient leader, always utilizing his resources as efficiently as possible. He was a stern but even-handed commander and his crew got along with him well. He knew that if he did find this missing celebrity his chances for promotion would be much better.

CHAPTER 21
DAY 2   7:00 AM

Ron woke up slowly, not remembering where he was. He opened his eyes to see the yellow life raft above his head. Now he remembered. He was still slightly wet but it was almost daylight and getting quite warm. He looked over at the women. They were all still asleep. He turned to Stanley. Stan was not breathing and had no pulse. He had died during the night. The shark bite must have severed the large artery in his leg and he had bled out before Ron could apply the tourniquet. Damn it. Ron crawled out from under the life raft. It was early morning and the sun was just slightly above the eastern sky. He stood up and walked over to the lagoon. He did not see the plane. It had disappeared.

The left wing tip showed just slightly above the surface of the lagoon, maybe a foot of the wing tip showing. It was the left side which had the intact float still attached. There was a sand beach about 30 yards from the tree line to the water. He looked at the other parts of the atoll. Looking to his left, there were maybe five groups of higher land areas with dense palm trees and brush growing on them separated by thin strips of sand. Looking to his right he saw a deeper passage from the outside ocean into the lagoon. That explained the presence of the sharks.

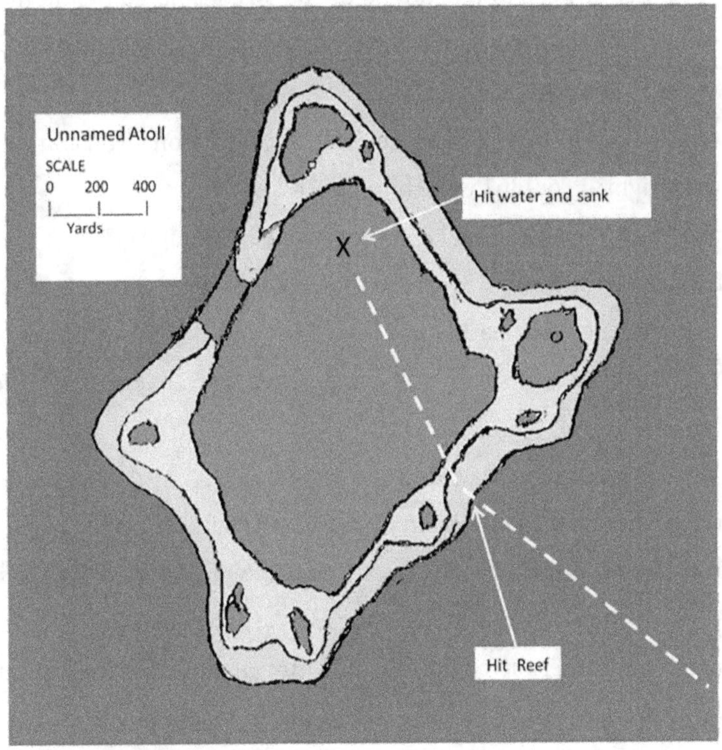

The lagoon itself appeared to be quite shallow, maybe 20 to 25 feet deep at the center and tapered up to the sand beach areas. He walked toward the island and looked at the palm trees. They were quite dense and several coconuts were scattered on the ground, probably knocked loose from the windstorm. There was a thick underbrush surrounding the palm trees. He walked across to the beach on the ocean side. The water between the beach and the coral reef was quite shallow up to the coral reef, probably only 4 or 5 feet deep. Waves were breaking on the reef, splashing over into the shallow water. He could see fish and crabs in the water. He walked back to the life raft. The women were stirring. Sylvia was in a lot of pain still with the broken arm. He could see that she would need to have some sort of a splint on that arm. Taylor was standing next to the raft. She turned to him.

"My cell phone has no signal," she complained to him.

"Do you see any cell towers out here?" he asked, amazed that in the rush to get out of a sinking plane she had remembered to grab her cell phone.

"How am I going to communicate?" she pleaded.

"You will have to wait until we get back to civilization," Ron commented. "Is Stan alright? I couldn't wake him," she asked Ron.

"I'm sorry but he didn't make it," Ron replied. "You mean?"

"He's dead. He must have lost too much blood," Ron said gently. "Oh my god," she said, her eyes tearing up.

"I need to bury him soon. It is going to get hot today and," he did not continue.

"They will rescue us today, won't they?" she asked.

"Well…I hope so. The problem is that the aircraft sank in the lagoon and the transponder probably won't work underwater," Ron tried to explain.

"I thought you knew how to fly a plane?" she asked harshly.

"We ran out of fuel and couldn't avoid hitting the reef," he tried to explain.

"You really screwed us up," she yelled and walked away from him. She immediately felt bad for yelling at him. He had tried to help them and she was blaming him for their situation. She turned and looked at him. He was walking away with his head down.

Ron had no answer for her anger so he went to the raft tent and pulled Stan out. In this heat he would have to bury him pretty quickly. He lifted Stan over his shoulder and carried him up the hill to the ocean side of the tree line. God, but he was heavy. Carrying the body was awkward and he stumbled a couple of times, but he managed to get to the top of the hill somehow. There was no soft ground for a grave at the top of the hill so he walked to the other side of the palms and dropped him on the ocean side beach close to the trees. He looked around and found a piece of wide flat drift wood and started to dig a shallow grave. He got it about two feet deep and decided that would have to do for now. He searched through Stanley's pockets and found a 3-inch folding pocket knife, a cigarette lighter and the five-shot .38 caliber revolver with four bullets and with one spare auto load clip with five rounds. He also had a handkerchief and a wallet with about two hundred dollars in cash, a few coins, credit cards and a license to carry a gun. There was also an auxiliary police badge from Orange County, California pinned to the inside of the wallet. He rolled Stan into the shallow grave and covered him with sand. He took the revolver and spare ammo clip and wrapped it in the handkerchief and buried it a few inches deep at the base of the tree closest to the grave. He pushed the piece of driftwood into the sand to mark the grave.

"Sorry buddy, I don't know the words," Ron muttered. He walked to the other side of the hill and saw that all of the women were awake and walking around. He walked up to Taylor and handed her Stan's wallet. She took it and looked at him.

"I'm sorry I yelled at you," she said with a tear rolling down her cheek. "You were trying to help us and didn't ask for this."

"I am sorry for Stan," Ron said. "I am an engineer, not a doctor."

"I suppose we should officially introduce everyone," Taylor replied. "I am Taylor Smith and that is my mother, Sara. The one with the broken arm is Sylvia, my agent, and the pretty girl with the bruised forehead is my best friend Betty."

"I am Ron, Ron Pritchard. I am an aerospace engineer," he introduced himself. The girls were still wearing the same outfits they had on the plane but were wet and wrinkled. He saw that the one called Sylvia was in a lot of pain. "We need to get that arm in a splint." He walked over to Sylvia.

"It really hurts a lot," Sylvia said cradling her arm with the other. "Do we have any coffee? I am dying for a cup of coffee."

"Is there any food?" Betty asked. "I'm hungry."

Ron walked over to the life raft. Sometimes these things had first aid kits in a pocket. He found the pocket but it was empty. He looked out at the lagoon. There might be one in the plane. He wished he had paid more attention to what was in the small galley on the plane before he left it.

"I'll go over to the plane and see what I can find," Ron said. "See if there is any coffee," Sylvia implored.

"You are going to swim back to the plane?" Taylor's mother, Sara asked, horrified. "What about the sharks?"

"I guess I will have to take my chances." Ron replied. "We need a first aid kit and there might also be some food on the plane." He got out the pocket knife he took from Stanley and looked at it. It was only 3 inches long when opened. He wondered if that would penetrate a shark's rough sandpaper-like hide. He rolled the pant legs of his jeans up past his knees. He took off his shoes and shirt and set them aside up on the beach. He waded out into the water while the four women watched. At least it was daylight this time and he should be able to see the sharks. He started to swim to the plane, occasionally looking around and below him. There were a couple of small sharks swimming near the bottom but they did not pay any attention to him. The lagoon was fairly shallow, only about 20 feet deep at the center. He got to the top part of the left wing and took a huge breath and then pulled himself down to the entrance hatch. The plane was perpendicular in the water, the left wing sticking upward and the starboard wing buried about 2 feet in the sand at the bottom of the lagoon. He saw that the right float was missing, probably torn off in the crash. He held his breath and looked around. He saw the same couple of small sharks swimming nearby but again, they did not seem to pay any attention to him. He got to the entrance hatch. It was closed. He thought he had left it open. He managed to open the hatch and some air bubbles went to the surface. He pulled himself in and found an air pocket inside the airplane, about six inches from the top of the left side of the fuselage. *Thank God,* he thought, as he took a breath of air. He worked himself toward the cockpit. He stopped in the small galley between the cockpit and main cabin and looked around. There was some dim light coming in from the aircraft windows, enough that he could see in the inside gloom. He saw a small first aid kit! He looked in the cockpit and saw a cooler floating near the pilot's seat. He grabbed it and put the first aid kit in it. It already had three cans of beer in it but there was room for four bottles of water from the refrigerator and what looked like some energy snack bars. They had plastic wrappers so they might still be good. He put these in the cooler also. He went into the cockpit again and found his carry-on bag. He transferred the snacks he had in the bag into the cooler. Hopefully the snack bars were still good after being in seawater. Looking around he saw something under the pilot's seat. It looked like a fancy cell phone. He put it into the cooler which was now quite full. He headed back toward the hatch. His carry-on bag had floated near the rear seats. He opened it and grabbed his small shaving kit with his medicines and tooth brush and put it in the cooler also. It was now full so it was time to leave. He took a big breath of air and went through the hatch. He came face to face with what looked like about a six-foot long reef shark. He jabbed the knife at it and it turned away. He noticed that the hatch closed behind him when he exited. He carefully swam back to the shore. The shark followed but did not attack. He touched bottom and walked out of the water. The women all rushed to him.

"We saw a big shark and thought he got you." Sara exclaimed. "You didn't surface for air so we thought…," she did not continue.

"There was an air pocket inside the plane," he explained. "Thank God you are safe," Sara said.

"Did you find anything?" Taylor asked, looking at the cooler.

"Yes there were some snacks and water bottles." He handed out the energy bars and the water bottles to the women. Ron gave Sara the cooler. He kept one water bottle. He took the first aid kit and his shaving kit and went over to Sylvia. She was still in some pain, cradling her arm. He looked around the beach until he found a couple of short straight lengths of driftwood that could be used as a splint. He had Sylvia sit on the sand and he got some tape from the first aid kit and taped the driftwood to her arm. He was as careful as possible to keep the bones straight. He wanted the bones aligned so it would knit together evenly. Luckily it was a simple fracture. It was a crude splint but it would have to do.

"Thank you." Sylvia said, somewhat relieved. Ron opened his small shaving kit.

He had a bottle of aspirin in it and he took out two and gave them to Sylvia.

"Here. This may help the pain. It's aspirin." He gave her the water bottle so she could take a drink and swallow the aspirin.

"Thank you." Sylvia smiled at him.

The others had already eaten most of the snack food. He managed to save some of it. "We might be here for a while; we probably need to ration this out." Taylor walked over to him. "Don't you think they will find us today?" she asked.

"I sure hope so, but I am not sure they know where to look. It could be a couple of days or more." He did not want to upset her. With the plane's transponder under water, it was doubtful that it was sending out any signals.

"These clothes are not going to last in this weather." Taylor noted. It was already getting hot and it was not even noon yet. "I cannot be out in this sun without my sun screen or sunglasses," she complained. "I will burn to a crisp in this sun."

"I suggest you stay in the shade of the palm trees for now. I need to check out the other small islands to see what I can find," he said. She looked at him coldly. She was not used to being ignored or not getting her way. Betty walked over to them holding the satellite phone she found in the cooler. "This looks like a satellite phone!" she exclaimed.

He had forgotten about that funny looking cell phone. He took it from her and tried to turn it on. It came on, but the battery symbol was blinking. It was almost dead. He did not know what frequency to set it to, so just pushed the transmit button. It automatically connected to the last number dialed. "Hello, hello, Hello," he said. "Mayday, I repeat Mayday. Our plane has crashed at an atoll in the Pacific, probably about two hundred miles west of Bora Bora. Please send help." He stopped the transmission. The screen dimmed and then went blank as the battery ran out.

"Do you think anyone heard it?" Taylor asked excitedly.

"I don't know," Ron said. "Let's hope so." He started to walk to the other end of the atoll.

The women huddled together under the shade of the palm trees. They removed their wet clothes and hung them on some bushes to dry. That left them just wearing their underwear. The temperature was already climbing into the eighties so they were not cold anymore.

"What do you think of him?" Betty asked Taylor.

"I don't know yet. He seems to be trying to be nice but it could be an act." Taylor was always suspicious of people she didn't know. In her line of work people were always trying to get something from her or use her somehow.

"He is wearing a wedding ring." Betty noted.

"That doesn't mean anything. Most married guys cheat anyway." Taylor responded.

"Well, he fixed my arm," Sylvia said. "He seems really nice." "He is sort of handsome…for an older man," Betty added. "He isn't that old. I think he is ok," Sara interjected.

"We shall see," Taylor said. "I really hope we get rescued soon." She did not trust anyone and her bodyguard was dead. She did not know this guy. He might be alright or maybe a serial rapist killer.

CHAPTER 21
DAY 2   11:00 AM

Snake Caputo was on board his cabin cruiser at the dock in Maupiti. There was no word about the missing plane. The news services were really making a big thing of it since the singer Taylor Smith was on the plane. He heard his satellite phone ring. He picked it up. He looked at the screen. It read 'Teddy'. He pushed receive and heard: "*Hello, Hello, Hello…. Mayday, I repeat Mayday. Our plane has crashed at an atoll in the Pacific, probably about….*" Then it cut off.

"Hello!" he shouted into the phone. "Hello…you are cutting out. Repeat!"

There was no response. Caputo looked at the phone. The other end had shut off. Why didn't they answer him? It was a man's voice, definitely not Teddy. At least he now knew that the plane had crashed at an atoll, but which one? He went into the cabin and spread out a chart of the Society Islands, one of which was Bora Bora. He knew they were not on Tupai. If they had crashed on an inhabited atoll, it would have been in the news already. So, it must be uninhabited. He knew that they flew west from Tupai so he looked at that end of the chart. There were only three other atolls on the chart. One was Motu One, two others were Manuae and Maupihaa. All of these were technically uninhabited. Motu One was one of the smallest atolls. The island atoll Manuae he knew to be deserted. The Maupihaa atoll had been populated by occasional science groups but was also now deserted.

So, he had three possible choices. Motu One was 550 kilometers from Tahiti so it was the farthest away. He decided they would look at Maupihaa first. He made sure that the boat was refueled and well provisioned. He looked out into the harbor. Both the French coast guard vessel and an even larger US Navy vessel had docked early this morning to coordinate a search plan. They would not have the new information he had just received about the atoll so he had a distinct advantage. He would beat them to the crash site. His attitude began to improve. He could almost count the money.

CHAPTER 22
DAY 2   11:15 AM

Ron decided to check out the other parts of the atoll. He walked along the sand spit between the small islands. It was getting hot so he removed his shirt and wore it around his head like an Arab headdress to keep the sun off his neck. He still had his shoes so he put them on to go exploring. He noticed that most of the women had lost their shoes when they swam to the island last night, with the exception of Sara who had tied-on sneakers. When he got to the island at the eastern end of the atoll, he climbed the small hill covered with coconut palms and underbrush. It was about a hundred yards long and quite dense with a lot of under growth and bushes. As he got to the top of the small hill he came upon a pool of water about a foot deep and around 10 yards in diameter. He knelt down and tasted the water. It was fresh water, probably deposited in this volcanic depression by last night's storm. Well, they at least had water, he thought. The first rule of survival was to find water. He walked to the edge of the island where the sand beach separated the palm growth from the sea. The coral reef apparently completely surrounded the atoll. He could see small fish in the shallow water leading up to the reef. He wondered if they were edible. The four women would soon be hungry and would look to him to find food. Jesus, he never expected to be marooned on a deserted island with a group of beautiful women. Each one of them was extremely beautiful.

Some men would consider this a fantastic opportunity, but his engineering mind could only see problems that had to be solved. He continued to walk around the atoll and there were four or five smaller outcrops of palm trees with smaller groups of dense bushes but that was it. There was no sign that anyone had ever been on the island. The only sign of civilization was the assorted plastic trash that had washed over the reef and up on the beach. Most of the plastic debris that had washed up on the beach side toward the ocean, consisted of mostly empty water bottles and plastic wrappers. He wondered if this island was even on the charts. The highest point was on the western island where they had swum to, but it was only about forty or fifty feet above sea level. Either this was a new atoll or was so low as to not be observed by ships passing. He made a complete tour of the atoll but then turned back west to the island where the women were. The women were trying to stay in the shaded area under the palm trees. The sun was beating down from directly overhead. It must be almost 90 degrees, Ron thought. The girls had stripped off their blouses and shorts to dry in some bushes and were in their bras and underwear. They tried to cover themselves with their hands as he approached.

"We need our clothes." Taylor said as he approached them.

"I was going to retrieve the suitcases from the plane anyway," he said, trying not to look at them in their underwear. He had already rolled up his pant legs to above his knees. He still had his undershirt on but removed the shirt from his head. He went back to the beach, removed his shoes, and waded into the water. He still had the 3-inch pocket knife to protect against sharks. He did not see any in the water but they were probably down there somewhere. He started to swim to the plane. Looking around and below, he did not see any sharks. He reached the plane without incident. The plane was almost perpendicular in the water with the left wing pointing straight up. He held his breath and pulled himself along the fuselage until he came to the luggage compartment. There was no handle that he could see but there was a slot for some sort of large T- shaped key. He turned around and found the entrance hatch and went into the plane. There still was a large air pocket on the left side of the plane and he breathed some air gratefully. He was sure he had seen the pilot using some sort of T-handle type key when his bag was being loaded. He looked around the cockpit and galley but could not see anything resembling the key. Then he remembered that they had put the dead pilot at the back of the plane. He moved to the back and found the pilot floating face down in the water. Ron figured that Ted was going to get pretty ripe soon but did not relish trying to pull him back to the beach with all of the sharks in the water. He searched the pilot's pockets and found the key. He also found a small automatic pistol tucked into Ted's belt. *Why the heck would he have a gun?* Ron wondered. He removed the pistol and shoved it into one of his back pockets. He also found a small Swiss army knife and a cigarette lighter. He put the items in one of his front pockets. He worked his way back to the entrance hatch and exited the cabin, closing the hatch.

He surfaced for a breath of fresh air and then moved down the fuselage to the luggage compartment. He was able to open it with the key and was relieved to see that it stayed open. He looked around but did not see any sharks. He grabbed one suitcase and started to swim to the shore. When he got to the shore, he deposited the suitcase where the women could see it and waded back in again. After about five more trips he had gotten most of the luggage ashore. He still had to find his suitcase with the steel urn container of ashes so he went back again. When he got to the plane he again went to the luggage compartment and looked for his suitcase. It was lodged way in the back and he had to reach blindly into the compartment and grabbed what he thought was his suitcase. Instead, he had a black plastic container with something in it. He swam back to shore with it. Maybe it was something that belonged to the women? He got to the shore and threw it up on the sand. He swam back to the plane. He was getting tired and was not sure he could make another trip but he just had to retrieve his wife's ashes. Finally, he did get his suitcase and swam back to the beach. He was so tired that he did not even look for the sharks this time.

The women were happy to get their clothing and personal items. A couple of suitcases had leaked and they hung their clothing to dry on the bushes surrounding the western island. Ron was tired but used this time to dig a slot in the sand into the hillside with a piece of driftwood. Then he arranged the yellow life raft like a tent between the palm trees. It shaded the slotted area from the noonday sun. Since the area was cut into the hill, it would be a good place for the women to sleep since it would be out of the wind and rain. What Ron found to be interesting was there did not appear to be any mosquitos or flies on the atoll. He thought that mosquitoes were all through the tropics, causing malaria. Apparently, there was no wildlife on the island, not even birds, so the female mosquitoes could not find any blood to suck to allow them to make eggs. The only form of life on shore was the palm trees and the thick underbrush. Possibly this atoll was relatively new, he thought. It was only about forty feet high at the top of the hill, which meant that since it had no mountain, passing ships could not see it until they were close. The women would need to go to the bathroom but there was a lack of any facilities on this island. He found a large piece of driftwood and started to look along the beach where some bushes would create some privacy and dug a latrine trench about twelve inches deep and about eight feet long. He now was getting very tired so he found a shady spot under a palm tree and took a nap.

CHAPTER 23
DAY 2   11:30 AM

Captain Anderson of the USS Preble scanned the seas with his binoculars. They had just launched the search helicopter and were patrolling the sea area just west of Bora Bora. He knew that they were looking for a two-engine amphibian aircraft, but if the pilot was dead, the aircraft could have crashed at sea. So, they had to look for any debris to possibly find some survivors. The tropical storm during the past night was making the search more difficult as the aircraft could have been blown off course before it went down. He knew that if any survivors were in the water, they must be found soon or they could possibly die from exposure or sharks. The helicopters made the search better but they were not getting any transponder signals so that meant that the aircraft was possibly under water. His commanding officer at Pearl had informed him that an important celebrity was on the downed aircraft and must be found as soon as possible. He did not care anything about the celebrity; he was just interested in rescuing any of the survivors. A French coast guard cutter and a French ATL2 maritime patrol aircraft were also searching the areas west of Bora Bora. The French ATL2 aircraft were typically stationed near the Atlantic Ocean but this one happened to be visiting French Polynesia. Captain Anderson had informed the French Government that he was in the area and would assist in the search. The French were somewhat surprised by his arrival but were happy to have the assistance. So, the French were searching the sea area toward the south while he was assigned the area to the north. Both groups were working their way westward from Bora Bora. The Captain of the Preble had looked up the type of plane they were looking for. It was an old Grumman G73 Mallard Sea plane with dual radial Pratt & Whitney engines. It had a range of about 1100 nautical miles. If the plane had full fuel tanks when it left Papeete, it could already be half way to Australia before it ran out of fuel. That was assuming that it did not go down in the storm. This made the search that much more difficult, but Captain Anderson was determined to put his best effort into finding the wreckage. The French had told him that the mayday message they had received said that the pilot had died and that they were about to crash. So that explained why it had not landed per its flight plan. What of the co-pilot? Somehow it did not make sense, but perhaps there was only the pilot? If no one knew how to fly the plane, it probably ran out of fuel and crashed into the sea. So, any survivors would have been in the water as the storm hit. That did not sound good. They probably were not going to find anyone. At least not anyone still alive.

CHAPTER 23
DAY 2   2:45 PM

Snake Caputo was on the bridge of his cabin cruiser looking at the atoll. Maupihaa was a fairly large U-shaped atoll. He scanned the island with his binoculars but only saw beach, palm trees and undergrowth. The plane could have crashed in the lagoon, so they approached with caution.

"I know there was at least one survivor since he called on the satellite phone." He spoke to Arno who stood next to him.

"We have to be careful of the reef surrounding the island. There is a passage on the south side but it is hard to find," Arno informed him. Arno was something of a giant. At six-foot six inches tall, he had become a weight lifter and was very powerfully muscled. He was dedicated to Caputo who had saved him from a life of poverty. He had become Caputo's lieutenant by his devoted service. He also had a black belt in karate and was a trained killer with a knife.

They both knew that this island was often visited by islanders and tourists, so there were a couple of small buildings on the island. The dense tropical growth was almost impenetrable but they would need to search the island thoroughly. If the plane actually crashed into the jungle, the passengers might be badly injured. If the singer was dead, he still had to at least recover his package of drugs.

"Find the passage through the reef." He commanded his crew. "I want to anchor in the lagoon and start searching the island as soon as possible."

CHAPTER 25
DAY 2   3:00 PM

Ron was exhausted from all of the work. He lay on the beach under a palm tree, trying to regain some strength. The women had retrieved their baggage and seemed happy to have their suitcases. They had all changed into bathing suits. Most of their stuff was wet so they had draped a lot of stuff on the underbrush to dry. It made for a colorful display. If a passing boat came by it would be hard not to notice. Taylor came over to him.

"We need more food and the water is all gone." She looked down at him on the beach as if he was her servant. She was wearing a bright blue bikini swimsuit and now had sandals on. She had also recovered a large beach hat and her sunglasses.

"Bring the empty water bottles and we will fill them up at a place I found," he told her. He reluctantly got up. She went back and gathered up six of the empty water bottles. He went and looked at his suitcase. He still had a mission to get to Bora Bora to spread Sue's ashes. One other carry-on bag was where he had left it. It must belong to Stanley. What was curious was what was in the black plastic bag. It did not appear to belong to anyone. He walked over to it and opened the bag. Inside were two white bags with what looked to be powder inside.

"What is that stuff?" Taylor asked as she approached him.

"I am not sure," Ron responded as he tried to open one of the white bags. "It looks like a bag of drugs, similar to what I have seen on TV newscasts," he stated.

"Oh my God," Taylor exclaimed. "What are we going to do with it?"

"I don't know, but this looks like it is worth a lot of money. The people it belongs to will be very eager to get it back," Ron replied. He figured that Ted's charter company was doing more than just transporting people to Bora Bora. He closed the bag and walked up to the underbrush and hid it under a bush.

"Are you going to just leave it there?" Taylor asked.

"I will bury it somewhere else later," he replied. "Come on, I'll show you where we can get some water." He started walking along the beach to the other island at the east end of the Atoll. Taylor followed him, wondering if he was leading her away from the others for some more sinister purpose. Ron looked at her in her bathing suit and smiled. She was really a sexy woman and he could not help but having some lewd thoughts. But he was not going to do anything to upset her.

"Thank you for getting our bags from the plane," Taylor said as she walked alongside of Ron. She was trying to make conversation since she did not know what type of person Ron was. Images of an aggressive single adult male alone with four vulnerable women on a deserted island flew through her mind. She wondered if he was going to take advantage of them.

"That's ok," he replied. "I had to retrieve my wife anyway." "Your wife?" She was confused.

"Yeah, she died of cancer 2 months ago and I promised I would spread her ashes on the beach in Tahiti. I have her funeral urn in my suitcase," Ron said looking down.

"You came all the way out here just to do that?" Taylor was shocked.

"Yeah . . . We really had a pretty good marriage for 25 years and her last words to me were that she regretted that we never made the trip to Tahiti." They were almost at the eastern island.

"Wow. That is pretty amazing. You must have really loved her a lot," Taylor noted that he had tears in his eyes.

"Yeah, I was always too busy with my work to take her to the one place she wanted most to visit, and then when we finally made plans to go she came down with cancer." He wiped the tears from his eyes. "Right up here ahead I found a pool of fresh water." He walked up the hill to the eastern island. There were a lot of coconut palms and underbrush. They picked their way through the underbrush and found their way to the pool. He knelt down and started to fill the water bottles.

"Is it big enough to take a bath?" Taylor asked.

"This is all the fresh water we have on this atoll. So, I think we should preserve it for drinking only," he stated.

She looked at him. "Ok, right. What are we going to do for food? Those energy bars you had did not last very long. The girls are already hungry back there," Taylor noted.

"Well, we do have coconuts," he said, screwing the tops back on the water bottles. He was already alarmed that the pool had shrunk somewhat due to evaporation. "This water is residue from the storm last night. It won't last very long I am afraid." He looked at Taylor. She was very beautiful and sexy wearing that bikini, he thought. But she needed to understand that if they were to survive they would need to conserve water.

"How long can we survive on coconuts?" she asked. She was used to eating in the best restaurants and typically did not have to worry about food. She was typically a salad person since she knew that her slim appearance and sexy looks were a major key to her career success.

"I'm not sure. Maybe we can catch some fish," he replied as he got up and started back to the western island.

"Do you know how to fish?" she asked, following him and carrying a couple of the water bottles.

"When I was a small child, my grandfather took me fishing once just before he died. How hard can it be?" he asked, wondering how to do it without any fishing poles or lines or hooks. They walked back to the others.

"Did you find water?" Sara, Taylor's mother asked as Ron passed out the water bottles to the others. Sara also was in a bathing suit also but it was a one-piece red suit and she wore shorts also. Ron noted that she was also very sexy in the bathing suit. He figured that she was about his age.

"Yes, there is a small pool at the other island but there is not much water there." Ron replied. "We need to conserve the water as long as we are here. I don't know how long it will take them to find us."

"So, we are stuck here?" Sylvia remarked. "What about our schedule? We will miss out on the videotaping!" she exclaimed.

"Look. Right now, we just need to think about surviving." Ron tried to calm her down. "I want to get out of here as much as you do, but we need to be thinking about long term survival until someone finds us. I really do not know where in the Pacific we are. It might be a good idea to gather up some driftwood and build a fire tonight. Someone might see it and alert the Coast Guard. I want you all to find as much drift wood as you can and pile it up near the tree line." Ron ordered. He figured if he gave them a task it would take their minds off of being hungry.

"What are you going to do?" Betty asked.

"I am going to try to catch us some dinner," he said as he picked up a long straight piece of driftwood and sat under a palm tree and started to cut a sharp point in the end with the knife he had taken off of Stanley. When the women started to talk to each other and walk away, he took out the small pistol he had taken from Teddy. It was a small Ruger .380 caliber pistol with four rounds in the magazine and one in the receiver ready to shoot if the trigger was pulled. It was so small, one could hide it in a pants pocket and it could not be detected. Sort of a useless weapon unless you were five feet away from what you were shooting at. He put it back in his pocket. *Maybe I could use it to kill a shark?* He thought. He took out the Swiss army knife. It had two small knife blades, a corkscrew, a small screw driver and a nail file. *This could come in handy*, he thought. He worked on the spear in earnest since he was starting to get hungry too.

It was a crude spear but the point was sharp. If he could get close enough to a fish maybe he could spear it. He grabbed the cooler. It still had three cans of beer in it. He hid them under a bush and proceeded to the ocean side of the island. He saw a bunch of coconuts laying on the ground. He wondered, how hard was it to eat one?

Chapter 26
Day 2   3:40 PM

Snake Caputo was becoming frustrated. His men had searched the Maupihaa island atoll and found no evidence of any wreckage or the survivors. There was evidence that some local natives had visited the atoll recently but they had probably left before the storm hit. He even had Arno snorkel dive in the lagoon to see if the plane was there. No such luck. He went into the cabin of the boat and took out the chart of the Society Islands again. The next island atoll to check would be Manuae.

A French search plane had flown over the island and circled a couple of times. The plane radioed him and asked if he had seen any evidence of a missing seaplane. He replied that he had not. When they asked him what he was doing at Maupihaa Island he replied that he was just a tourist and doing some fishing. That appeared to satisfy the aircraft and it flew away. Since most of his crew members were on the island searching through the dense jungle foliage, the aircraft did not spot anyone carrying weapons.

If they did not find anything here, they would go to Manuae. Manuae was an atoll consisting of two large islands. It was a protected conservation park for sea turtles and shore birds and was uninhabited. Caputo knew that there was a park station on the island but it was only used when it was visited by a tourist boat. He doubted that any tourist excursions would be there at this time of year but he would have to make sure when he got there. As soon as his crew got back on board they would head for Manuae Island. The survivors probably had to be there since that island was closest to the route the plane was traveling.

The remaining atoll, Motu-One was a very small atoll which Caputo knew was also uninhabited. If they weren't on Manuae, then they would have to be at Motu-one. He had to find the survivors before the coast guard found them. At least he did not have to search the ocean carefully, which the coast guard had to do. Time was on his side for the moment.

CHAPTER 27
DAY 2   4:00 PM

On the USS Preble, Captain Anderson was talking to Lieutenant Olsen, one of the helicopter pilots. Lieutenant Olsen was a young African American Annapolis graduate, who had excelled in flying helicopters. He had just landed on the afterdeck of the ship after scouting ahead for a search radius of about 50 miles. The other helicopter had not returned yet.

"No sign of any wreckage or debris. They must have crashed much further west." Olsen stated as he reported to the captain.

"Well, I want you to take a break, but get the helo refueled and get back up there as soon as you are able." Captain Anderson was afraid of this. If the seaplane had enough fuel, it could have covered a longer flight path and they were possibly searching too close to Bora Bora. He did not want to assume that and possibly miss the wreckage if it was close by, so he was forced to search the area thoroughly. He ordered the engine room to increase speed and kept the lookouts in place, just in case. He wondered if the French were having any better luck. He had not heard from them since this morning, so probably not.

A message from the Admiral at Pearl Harbor asked if they had found the survivors yet. He reluctantly radioed back that the small charter aircraft had not yet been found. The news stations on the US mainland were covering the story repeatedly and probably would continue until the famous pop singer was found. More assets were coming to aid in the search, several coast guard cutters from Hawaii and a Navy Nuclear Sub were also heading this way. Captain Anderson was hoping that the wreckage would be found soon. The longer any survivors were in the water the less chance of survival. He called the radio operator on the intercom.

"Sparks, radio Pearl that we need the latest satellite photos of the area west of Tahiti. I want them to re-task the satellite if necessary and give us a 500-mile radius around Tahiti," he ordered.

"Sir, the satellite over Pearl is required to be in place for National Security reasons. I don't think they will want to re-task it." Sparks answered.

"Just make the call," he replied. "I don't think we are going to get a surprise attack from the JAPs today." Having the satellite photos would help the search immensely. "If necessary, call the Admiral to make the request." He hung up. The US Government had a geo-synchronous satellite over Pearl Harbor to watch the island area for security purposes. It would not hurt anything to have it moved slightly to photograph the area around Tahiti.

CHAPTER 28
DAY 2 4:15 PM

Ron had found several coconuts on the ground in the palm tree area. They probably had fallen during the high winds in the storm last night. He did not know how to tell if any of them were ripe or not. He struggled to remove the husk of a coconut. He had seen natives remove the husk with their teeth on National Geographic programs about Hawaii. It sure was not the same with these coconuts. Finally, he was able to free the small round coconut. He tried to cut a hole in the coconut with the pocket knife but it was not easy. He finally gave up and found a small pointed rock and a larger flat rock and used it as a hammer on the small stone. His first attempt caused the coconut to shatter and he lost the coconut milk on the ground. This was not as easy as he had hoped. Still, the inside of the coconut was available to eat. He cut off a small piece and chewed it. It was not bad but very fibrous. He wondered what the nutritional value of the coconut was. Probably it was not enough to survive on. He ate a few more pieces to satisfy his hunger. He decided to leave and headed to the beach on the ocean side of the western atoll. He grabbed the cooler he had liberated from the plane and headed for the sea side. He had seen several fish swimming in the water area between the beach and the coral reef. With his sharpened driftwood spear, he might be able to spear a couple. As he waded into the water he saw the fish swim away from him. He needed to move slowly so as not to alarm them. He moved closer to the reef. The water was about five feet deep at this point so he ducked under the surface to get closer to the reef. A lot of fish were swimming around the reef and he even saw a small octopus retreating into a hole. Soon the fish were ignoring him and a couple came within range. The first ten or twelve attempts were unsuccessful as the fish were pretty fast. Finally, he managed to impale a large red colored fish. It was about eight inches long. He remembered reading about red colored animals being poisonous, but hoped that was not true for fish. He returned to the shore and took the fish and put it in the cooler, then started hunting for another victim.

He did not see Sara watching him from the bushes. She was curious about this man who had helped them escape the sinking plane. Her daughter had told her about his wife dying of cancer and his mission to spread her ashes in Tahiti. He was somewhat handsome and apparently a good swimmer. Now he was trying to catch some fish for her companions to eat. He was very calm in the aircraft when everyone else was screaming and in panic. He said he was an engineer so maybe that was why he was trying so hard to solve their problems. So far he had not asked for anything in return. She wondered if he was attracted to her. They were about the same age. She had stopped mourning over her dead husband months ago. She was happy to go on the trip to Tahiti with Taylor so she could start living her life again. She thought Ron was very nice and wondered if he liked her or not.

After about 2 hours Ron had speared four fish. He left the water when he saw a four-foot reef shark become interested in a fish he had speared. He wondered about killing a shark. Were they good to eat? He knelt near the shallow water and gutted the fish, cleaning them the best he could. This brought a lot of interest in some smaller fish who came close to scavenge the internals. He thought that maybe if he had a fishing line and a hook he could use this material as bait. After cleaning the fish, he walked back to the palm tree area where the women had gathered a respectable pile of driftwood. There was a huge rock about four feet high and three feet wide near where they had piled the driftwood. There was another large rock sticking out of the sand that was about four feet high and six feet long. It made for a good kitchen counter. He figured to start the fire next to the large rock. It would shelter the fire from the wind and act as a platform to prepare food. It was getting late and would be dark soon. It was time to cook the fish. They didn't have any pots or pans to cook with so he would have to just hold the impaled fish on a stick over the flames. Perhaps the girls liked sushi? Maybe they could eat the fish raw but he wasn't going to do that. Sara noticed that he had been successful fishing. "It seems like you found some food," she praised him as he walked toward them.

"Yeah, but I'm not sure how we will cook these babies," he replied.

"We have the wood but don't know how to start a fire," Betty complained. "Do any of you have any paper in your baggage?" Ron asked.

"Well, I do, but it is the contract for the video we are going to make," Silvia said. "Can I see it, please?" Ron asked.

"Why do you want it?" Silvia asked, defensively.

"Do you want to eat raw fish, or do you want it cooked?" Ron replied. "Go get the contract, Sylvia," Taylor ordered.

Silvia reluctantly retrieved the contract and gave it to Taylor who handed it to him. Ron looked at the document it was about 40 pages long and had dried out from being in the salt water. It was a little wrinkled but still readable.

"Do you have an electronic copy of this in a computer somewhere?" Ron asked. "Yes, but it is back in San Diego," Sylvia replied.

"Good," Ron said as he ripped the first three pages off and handed the remainder back to her.

"You can't do that!" Sylvia exclaimed.

"I just did," Ron replied. He took the paper and crumpled it up and put it at the bottom of a small pile of wood. He took one of the driftwood pieces and started to carve on it with the knife, making a small pile of wood shavings. He put this with the paper at the bottom of the pile, then took out the lighter he took off of Stanley and lit the paper. Soon the paper ignited the shavings and then he placed some wood on top of it. Finally, the drift wood began to burn. As the fire got bigger he piled on more of the wood until they had a pretty good bonfire going. He then cooked the fish on a wooden spit. He was not sure how long to cook it but as the fillets started to turn brown he figured it was done. He took the spit off the fire and let the fish cool a bit. He offered the first fish to Taylor who looked back at him in dismay.

"You expect us to eat that?" she asked. "Either this or go hungry," Ron noted.

"I'll try it," Sara said and took the fish and bit into it. "It's not bad," she remarked. "OK," Taylor took the next piece and sat next to her mother. She took a bite and smiled.

"I refuse to eat this," Silvia said. Betty did not hesitate and took the third fish and sat down next to Taylor.

"Suit yourself," Ron said as he slid the fourth fish off the stick. "Wait. I am really hungry," Silvia grabbed the last fillet.

"What are you having?" Sara asked Ron. He merely smiled at her and walked away. He still had one snack bar left and walked away into the brush to eat it. He walked over to bushes where he had placed his suitcase and opened it and took out the funeral urn. He sat there looking at the urn. He wondered what Susan would say about his predicament. She probably would tell him to do the best he could in the situation.

Ron had improved the lean-to for the women by tying the raft between two close palm trees. It was a lot more stable and would protect the women from the sun and wind. It was still large enough for all four women who had made beds in the groove out of some of their clothes from their suitcases. Earlier Ron also had dug a slit trench in the sand about 50 yards away from the encampment. It was situated between two sets of bushes, so it was somewhat private. He informed the girls that they could use this as a latrine but to cover their deposits with sand. They asked about toilet paper but he did not have an answer for that. He said to use whatever leaves from the foliage they could find. He did not think there was any poison ivy on a tropical island.

He had taken some driftwood to the ocean side of the island and lit a small bonfire that he hoped would be seen by a passing ship. He sat against a palm tree and watched the fire. He kept adding wood to keep it going, occasionally looking out to sea hoping to see a ship or aircraft. If a passing boat was within sight it would have lights. If there was a boat, they might just see the bonfire and come to investigate. He watched for a couple of hours but did not see anything. He was still hungry so he walked over to the bush where the cooler had been dumped out. There were still three cans of beer there. He grabbed one and opened the tab pull. He walked over and sat next to the fire. He sipped the beer. He was used to cold beer, but even this warm one tasted good. He watched the sea for a couple of hours, hoping to see the light of a passing boat but did not see one. He was really tired and finally fell asleep next to the fire.

CHAPTER 29
DAY 3   6:15 AM

Ron woke up with the first light. He was still wearing shorts and a T-shirt with his sneakers but it had not gotten too cold at night. The fire, however, had gone out during the night. He got up and scanned the horizon in all directions. There was still no sign of a ship or a plane. He thought that having a famous celebrity in the group would cause a massive search and rescue mission. Maybe later today they would be found. He went over to where he had hidden the drug bags and took them over to where he had buried Stanley. He dug a hole in the sand and buried the bags near the body. He did not want to speculate what would happen if the women started to use the drugs.

He started to think of something to do and decided to make a sign in the sand on the beach. He walked to the Lagoon side of the island. He gathered more driftwood and started to spell out 'HELP" with it in a clearing on the sand beach in front of the small island that they were staying on facing the lagoon. He had noticed some fallen palm trees that had been pushed over by the recent storm and pulled a couple of the smaller ones over to make the long legs of the "H" and the 'L.' He then cut some brush and filled out the 'E' and the 'P' It was not the best sign but it should be readable from the air.

Sara came over and watched him work. She was now in a one-piece blue bathing suit and wore some white sandals.

"Do you think it will help?" she asked.

"Well, it might. We need to do everything we can," Ron replied.

"Taylor told me about your wife," Sara said, helping him straighten out the top of the 'E'.

"Yeah, Susan died of cancer. It hit her so fast there was nothing the doctors could do," Ron replied.

"The girls have noticed that you haven't taken advantage of our situation. Four women trapped on a 'desert island' with a single man," Sara stated.

"What do you mean?" Ron asked.

"Some men would be somewhat aggressive in this type of situation," Sara looked at him. "We really do not know you at all, but you have built us a shelter, retrieved our clothes and provided food and water."

"I am an engineer. I have been trained to solve problems. We need food and water to survive so I am doing my best for everyone involved. I would never try to take advantage of a woman unless she wanted me to." He looked back at her. She was really sexy, he thought.

"That is nice to know. I bet you never cheated on your wife," Sara replied.

"Well, . . . that is true. I was totally in love with my wife. We had a special relationship that not many couples have," he said, returning to working on the sign.

"Yet you have sort of taken charge here," Sara looked down in the sand.

"Look. Someone has to try to get things done. I did not think of 'taking charge' that way. If you girls want to do things differently, let me know." He stopped working on the sign. It should read well from the air he thought.

"No. It appears they are willing to do things as you want. But they are suspicious of your motives." Sara stood back and looked at the sign.

"Well, you can tell them I am only interested in survival, nothing else." Ron walked up to her. "I realize that you are all beautiful women and I can't deny that I am very attracted to all of you, but I am not the type of guy to intrude where he is not wanted. They don't have anything to worry about, ok?"

"Well. Ok then." Sara was somewhat amazed by this man. He appeared to have a code of honor that she did not see in most men. They walked back to the encampment together. He gathered up the empty water bottles and started to walk over to the eastern island where the pool of water was. Sara walked over to talk to Taylor and Silvia. Betty got up and walked over next to Ron.

"You going to get more water?" she asked.

"Yeah, you girls are drinking a lot of water in this heat, but that is ok. In these temperatures you need to keep hydrated." It was already up in the high 80's he thought. The sky was clear and sun was beating down. "You should stay in the shade as much as possible or you might get sunburned," Ron said. Betty was wearing a red bikini and had a white blouse loosely covering her shoulders and back. She had also retrieved a wide brim straw hat from her suitcase and was wearing it. She had found some brown sandals in her luggage and was wearing them as well. He thought she was very sexy too.

"We want to thank you for the fish yesterday. It was really good," she said, trying to make conversation.

"I will try to get some more fish for lunch. I hope you guys like fish because I am not sure we have much else to eat here," Ron was himself getting hungry.

"Taylor tells me that you recently lost your wife," Betty noted

"Yes," he replied. He noted that he would have to watch what he said since the women seemed to talk to each other about everything.

"You brought her ashes out here to bury them?" Betty asked.

"Yes. We had always planned to travel to Tahiti and when we had finally made arrangements, she came down sick. So, I made a promise to bury her in Bora Bora." He was getting tired of explaining himself.

"Well that seems very noble. Taylor says she thinks you are very nice," Betty explained.

"I have heard her sing. She has some great songs. Isn't she engaged to some actor?" he asked.

"Yes. I believe he was going to fly out here to be with her after the photo shoot and video."

"Well, I hope we get rescued pretty soon so she can get back to her work," he said as they started to climb the hill to the eastern island. They got to the top and the pool was still there. He filled the water bottles and handed them to Betty to put the caps on. He noticed the pool was slightly lower, now only about 10 inches deep. He took a long drink of water from one of the bottles and re-filled it.

"We are pretty lucky you found this pool." Betty noted.

"Yeah, but unless we get another storm this will all evaporate in a few days." "What will we do then?" she asked.

"Well, if I figure out how to open coconuts properly, we will have coconut milk to drink."

"You are pretty smart, aren't you?" she asked.

"Not really. I am just trying to find ways to survive. Hopefully they will find us soon," he replied.

"That would be nice," she replied. "We will have had a real adventure to tell everyone about. That is what is killing me. I have not messaged my friends on Facebook for almost three days. How are we supposed to know what are our friends are doing?" she complained. "I just don't know what to do."

"Well, you just have to try to survive like the rest of us. Let's head back. I never use social media so I guess I don't miss it." He got up from the water hole and picked up the water bottles. "Really?" She was shocked. *How could anyone live without social media?* she thought.

"What will you do after we get rescued?" she asked as they started to walk back to the encampment. "Go back to Cleveland and resume my engineering job," he replied.

"Do you think I am pretty?" she asked before they got to the encampment "Definitely. You girls all look gorgeous to me."

"I wondered if you were going to try to take advantage of any of us. You haven't even flirted with anyone."

"Look. I already explained to Sara that I am not looking to do anything like that. We will get rescued soon and you all will be able to forget all this. I am not going to try to impose myself where I am not wanted," Ron replied.

"Oh," she said and walked over to the other women.

He placed the water bottles in the shade under one of the palms where the women could get to them. Then he picked up his spear and the cooler and headed for the outer island reef to find some fish. He was somewhat taken aback by the women's worries that he would take advantage of them. True, they were all beautiful, sexy and attractive and walking around in skimpy bathing suits did nothing to cool his reaction to them, but he was not going to take any advantages. He supposed that they were scared and paranoid. Anyone would be after what had happened to them here. They did not know him or what type of person he was. But he wasn't going to try anything with these women. He still felt faithful to his wife. He got to the ocean side of the atoll. He waded into the water and started to look for fish. He was slightly better at it today and caught six good sized fish. He would have to start the signal fire again tonight, but try to conserve driftwood. There was only a finite amount of driftwood that could be used for a fire. He wanted to light a fire again tonight as a signal beacon. He cleaned the fish with the knife and headed back to the small camp with the fish fillets in the cooler. He impaled the fillets on a stick as he had done before. The women were all sitting in the lean-to tent he had built with the life raft. He gathered up some driftwood and started the fire. They were all pretty quiet which was unusual. They usually were chatting among themselves constantly. He started cooking the fish as before. Sara came over and sat down beside him. He looked at her and said "These should be ready in a few minutes." "We have had a meeting about you," she said.

"Really?" He looked at her curiously.

"We want to know what you intend to do about getting us rescued."

"There really isn't much more I can do that hasn't already been done," he replied. "You are an engineer. Can you retrieve the radio from the plane and get it to work?"

"I used the radio when we were in the air and got no response." He looked at her.

"Exposure to the salt water will have corroded any of the electronics now that it is underwater," he explained. "I could go and try I suppose, but it would probably be a futile effort."

"Oh. I did not think of that," she replied.

"Ok. We need to talk." He put the fish down and walked with Sara over to the girls.

He sat down facing the others. "This is the way I see it," he stated calmly, "We left Papeete and flew west for about three and a half hours. At around 150 miles an hour, that puts us around 350 miles west of Bora Bora. I have scouted this atoll carefully and have not found any evidence that it has ever been visited before by humans. We are obviously off the normal shipping lanes since I have seen no lights of any ships passing in the night. We have a limited water supply and very little to eat except fish and coconuts. I want to be rescued just as bad as you do. I am sorry that the plane crashed upon landing, I suppose I am not a very good pilot after only two lessons. I am trying my best to help us survive. This being the case, we may be on this island for quite some time. I am hoping that they find us soon since most searches typically end after two to three weeks." He finished his speech, looking at them.

The girls nodded and Taylor stood up. "I believe you are doing everything possible you can do to help us. We might be stranded here for quite some time. I do not think they will give up on finding us that soon, at least I hope not. We just needed to hear you tell us what you think." She sat back down. Obviously she was the leader of the girls.

"Ok," he said. "Who wants a fish?" He walked back to the fire.

After everyone had a fish, he re-lit the signal fire on the ocean side. Sylvia followed him and he inspected her broken forearm. The splint was working well, the bones were still lined up ok. As long as she did not bump it, it should heal ok. He had made a sling out of one of her blouses by cutting a hole past the elbow and tying the sleeve to the collar. It ruined the blouse but looked like it would free up her other hand better.

"How did you know how to do that?" Sylvia asked.

"I didn't really know how… I just improvised. Sorry that the blouse is ruined now," he apologized.

"That's ok. Looks like you are part doctor too." She smiled at him.

"Not really. I know if we did not put a splint on that arm it would give you a lot of trouble later. It looks like everything will heal ok now . . . as long as you don't bump it. I have nothing here to make a cast for your arm." He looked at her eyes. She had beautiful eyes. He sort of blushed and moved away.

"Are you really that shy?" she noted.

"Not really, but all of you girls are so very beautiful, . . . but you are about the same ages as my daughters."

"Tell me about them." She asked.

"Alice is a nurse's aide at the Cleveland Clinic. She has always wanted to help people so she turned to nursing. Her mother and I are very proud of her. My daughter Sandra recently got married to a doctor and is living in Oregon. She also does volunteer work for the homeless. So, I guess they are both doing quite well," he explained.

"It sounds as if you raised them right," she replied.

"It wasn't me . . . I was gone on work trips most of the time. My wife Susan was the one who really raised them." As he looked down a tear formed in his eye.

"Well, . . . they must have had a strong father figure to help them too." Sylvia could tell that she had pushed him too far.

"Yes, . . . I better tend to the fire." He turned away and walked over to the fire wondering if he would ever see his daughters again. He built up the fire. Someone out on the ocean might see it. At least he hoped so.

CHAPTER 30
DAY 4   8:00 AM

Captain Anderson on the Preble had finally received the satellite photos he requested. The Admiral had to verify the request in order to get it done. There were several hundred high-definition images to review. He called Ensign Owens to the bridge.

"Ensign Owens reporting, sir," The young ensign saluted the captain.

"Owens, I want you to review all of the satellite photos we just received to look for a downed plane or survivors in the water. Report anything and I mean anything that could be a sign of the survivors. Get a chief petty officer to help you."

"Yes sir. I will get right on it." Owens walked away. *Jesus, I get all of the shit jobs*, he thought. He went down to the weapons control ready room where he could find the largest viewing screen and started to pull up the images from the satellite feed. He requested that Chief McCredie assist him since there was only one other viewing console that could be used. It looked like it was going to be a long day. The viewing screen allowed them to pull up each photo and magnify or enlarge small objects several times for close observation. Each satellite photo covered almost a square mile so the viewer had to search and pull up and magnify anything of interest. There were several hundred photos covering the area just around Tahiti. It took a long while just to review each one of the hundreds of photos. Chief McCredie suggested that they start at opposite ends of the photo collage and work toward the middle. Owens agreed and they started to work.

CHAPTER 31
DAY 4   9:00 AM

Ron was up early and went over to the ocean side where he fished. Yesterday he had left most of the fish internals on the area between the beach and water line. As he hoped, crabs came up to eat the fish scraps. He managed to catch four fairly good- sized crabs. He thought that a change in menu might brighten up the women's attitude. He put them in the cooler. He didn't think he could cook them on a spit like the fish. The women were all sort of depressed since they had been on the atoll for almost four days and had not been rescued yet. He pondered on how to cook the crabs. He needed a pot or something to boil them in. He looked at the lagoon and the plane's wing had slipped so that now only about six inches of the wing tip was now visible. He decided he was going to swim over and scour the small galley for something to cook the crabs in. He had dressed in his swim trunks that he recovered from his suitcase. As he waded into the water, Sara came over to say hello.

"What are you going to do?" she asked. She was wearing a yellow blouse with blue shorts and brown sandals. Apparently, their clothes had dried sufficiently to allow them to change outfits.

"I am going to see what I can scavenge from the plane." "Aren't there still sharks in the water?" she asked.

"Well, they haven't bothered me in the daylight. I am hoping that it will stay that way," he replied hopefully.

"Please be careful," she implored.

He started to swim over to the plane and saw one large reef shark, about six feet long, prowling along the bottom. It didn't seem to take notice of him. He got to the wing and took a large breath and worked his way down to the entry hatch. The shark came up to meet him and had an aggressive curve to its body. He had seen this type of behavior on some National Geographic television programs and realizing that the shark was about to attack, he quickly ducked into the cabin. The shark swam past and circled the opening. He looked for the pocket of air but it was now only about two inches from the side of the fuselage. He was able to get a breath and headed for the galley. He searched the cupboard but did not find anything useful. The paper plates and napkins were all in bad shape from being underwater. A screwdriver about eight inches long was also in the cupboard, next to a metal fork. He had not seen these before. He grabbed the fork and screwdriver and shoved them into his swim trunks. There was a small toaster oven attached to the side of the small refrigerator that he had ignored before. On an impulse, he opened the toaster oven and found an aluminum pan about 2 inches deep. *This might do to cook crabs,* he thought and he grabbed it. He got back to the air pocket and took another breath. As he leaned on the fuselage for support, he felt the plane position pitch to the right. The air pocket moved to the open hatch and bubbled up to the surface. So now he had no air and the shark was still out there. He saw the body of Teddy the pilot all bloated and white float by. Without thinking, he grabbed the body and shoved it out of the exit hatch. The body floated up toward the surface but was caught by the shark which began to tear it apart. He used this distraction to swim to the bottom of the lagoon and head for the beach. A couple of smaller sharks swam past him to join in the feast the large shark was having. He was sorry to have to do that to the pilot but it at least allowed him to escape. He finally broke the surface about 20 yards away and swam toward the beach. He looked back and the plane had tilted over and was now resting on its roof at the bottom of the lagoon. He got back to the beach ok. The sharks were noisily attacking the corpse of Teddy out on the surface of the lagoon. Sara was at the edge of the beach crying as he came out of the water behind her. She looked over, startled to see him.

"I thought that was you the sharks were attacking!" There were tears in her eyes. "No, I was lucky this time. I guess we won't have to bury Teddy," he reassured her.

"Thank God you are safe," she started to cry again.

"It's ok. I am sorry to get you worried." He was glad that she was concerned for him. They walked back to the camp and he showed her the pan he had risked his life for. They got back to camp and the other women were up but hungry. He asked if anyone had a hair dryer in their luggage. It turned out that Betty had one.

"Do you mind if I destroy this?" He asked Betty. She was wearing a skimpy red bikini and looked sexy as all get out.

"I suppose so, ... it isn't working for me here," she replied.

"Thanks." He took it from her and cut the cord off with the pocket knife. He took the pan he had retrieved and placed it against a palm tree for support, then took the screw driver and fashioned a slot hole in the side of the pan. He then took the Swiss army knife and used the corkscrew to make two holes next to the screwdriver slot. He then inserted the screw driver into the slot. Using the wires from the hair dryer he carefully stripped off the rubber insulation and used the bare copper wire to insert into the two holes and wrap around the wider tip of the screw driver and then used the excess wire on the outside to wrap around the shaft of the screwdriver outside of the pan. When he was done, they had a crude basic frying pan with plastic screwdriver handle.

Sara came over to inspect it. "Wow. You think it will work?"

"It should work if we are careful not to bang it around too much," he replied. He went to the beach and got some salt water in the pan. He could just fit two of the crabs in the pan. He stunned the crabs by hitting them on the large rock. He started the fire and cooked the crabs, turning them with the fork as they cooked. The women watched carefully and when the crabs were done, they had a feast. They did not have a nutcracker but the crab legs were easy enough to break apart. He cooked the other two crabs and tried some of it. It was not bad if you were hungry enough. He looked at the women again. He started to have lewd thoughts. It probably was only normal being around four very attractive and sexy women, all wearing nothing except skimpy bathing suits. Still, he was not one to force himself on a female. If one of them tried to seduce him though, she would probably be successful. He put the thought out of his mind.

After they had all eaten, he walked over to the lagoon and washed out his makeshift fry pan. He then walked over to the bush he had put the funeral urn under and took it out. He sat on the sand and held the urn tightly. He still felt that it was too soon to be thinking of other women instead of his wife Sue. He still missed her dearly. Sara walked over and sat next to him. "Is that the urn?" she asked in a low tone. "Yes, this is what is left of my Susan." He had a tear on his cheek.

"You are still devoted to her, aren't you?" "I guess so…I miss her so much it hurts," he confessed. They sat there in silence for a while. Then she turned to him.

"You need to let her go." Sara said. She put her arm around him to comfort him.

"I know." he replied.

CHAPTER 31
DAY 4   9:30 AM

Snake Caputo was on his boat at the atoll Manuae. The two islands making up the atoll were fairly large and he had his three gunmen with Arno get ready to go ashore in the skiff and search for the survivors. About that time a US Navy helicopter came over the boat and hovered over him. The radio crackled. Randy answered the radio and gave the microphone to Caputo.

"Ahoy on the boat. Have you seen any survivors or a float plane that may have crashed near here?" Lieutenant Olsen asked.

"No. We are just here fishing. We haven't seen a downed plane or any survivors." Caputo answered. The fishing ploy had worked before, it should work again.

"Ok. Thanks." The Navy Helicopter veered away.

"That's strange," Ensign Jones, the helicopter copilot said. "What?" Lieutenant Olsen asked.

"I am sure I saw those guys in the skiff holding machine guns."

"Really? Maybe we should go back and investigate. I didn't see any fishing gear on the deck of the boat. And did you see the name of the boat? It was *PIRATE*." Olsen hesitated. His mission was to find survivors, not interdict possible pirates. The island looked deserted anyway. He continued on with his search pattern. If there were any survivors on the atoll they would have come out of the trees and started waving as they heard the helicopter pass over. He headed over to the other island to look around. They passed slowly hovering about 20 feet off the ground, hoping that a survivor would come out and signal them. There was no sign of any crashed plane, but it could have crashed in the lagoon between the islands. After about a half hour they gave up. They were running low on fuel and had to return to the ship.

"Damn Navy pilots." Caputo said, watching the helicopter fly away. It looked as if the search for the celebrity singer was closing in. He needed to find the girl and his drugs quickly. The helicopter was flying over the atoll fairly low. If Teddy's plane had crashed in the trees, it should be visible from the air. He watched the helicopter carefully. He probably could not shoot it down with the small arms he had but if they landed to rescue any survivors he could sneak up on them and shoot the pilots as they exited the aircraft. Still, it was possible that the plane had crashed into the center of the atoll and sunk, leaving the survivors to swim for land. It had been three days now; they would be hungry and weak. So, he recalled his gunmen and watched the helicopter carefully through his binoculars as it passed over the two islands, stopping to hover now and then but not setting down. After the helicopter left, apparently not finding anything, Caputo realized that this must be the wrong atoll. Caputo was disappointed. If the Navy couldn't find them, they probably weren't on this atoll. Where the hell were they then? He considered doing a thorough search of both islands, but time was running out. He looked at his chart. There were no other atolls out here. Teddy's plane must have flown farther west than he thought. The only close island they had not searched was Motu- One. Possibly the man using the satellite phone had crashed landed there? It was at night and in a storm when they crashed, but why didn't he use the aircraft radio to keep transmitting after the crash? He also thought aircraft had automatic transponders in case they crashed.

Just in case the plane had crashed inside of this atoll and sunk, he had Arno put on his diving gear and go down to look. If the drugs were still on the amphibian, he had to retrieve them. The small delay to make sure was worth the time it took. He paced back and forth waiting for Arno. He went into the bridge of the boat and saw Captain Randy sitting, looking at the charts.

"Can we access the internet here with our satellite gear?" he asked Randy.

"Yes, . . .I think so. What do you want?" Randy replied.

"See if you can pull up Goggle maps of this area. We may be missing something that is not on the charts." Caputo was getting desperate. Arno surfaced and reported in.

"No plane down there," he said. "There are a lot of sharks though."

"Do you think we should search the island? The helicopter apparently did not see any sign of survivors or they would have landed on the beach to rescue them." Caputo asked him.

"I don't think they are here. But if they are, why would they hide from the helicopter?" Arno was taking off his diving gear.

"Well, we are running out of atolls to search," Caputo said, very frustrated.

"One of the local natives told me some time ago that there are other islands out here that are not on the charts. I didn't pay much attention to it since it did not seem important at the time." Arno stowed his gear in a nearby cabinet.

"Should we go and ask some of the natives?" Caputo asked.

"We could, but we would probably have to go back to Manupiti to find them.

"We don't have time for that." Caputo stood near the railing looking at the island. "The Navy is getting too close to finding them. We need to move fast. What about Motu- one?" he asked.

"They could be there, but it is a pretty small island." Arno replied.

"Well, we should make sure. Make course for Motu-one," Caputo commanded.

He had to beat the rescuers.

CHAPTER 32
DAY 4   NOON

Ron had piled up a bunch of coconuts. He had decided to try to try opening another coconut. This time he peeled off the husk and used the corkscrew from the Swiss army knife to make a hole in the coconut. He then gently used the knife to make the hole bigger. It seemed to work this time and he held the coconut up and let the milk drain into his mouth. It was not bad. Not as refreshing as water but not bad. Sara had been watching him from the bushes again and walked over. She was wearing the blue bathing suit with yellow shorts and the brown sandals.

"So, this is how you have been getting nourishment?" she asked, joking.

"It's not too bad. If we run out of water, I can start opening these up. There must be hundreds of them on this atoll," he smiled at her.

"We need to fill these again." She showed him a handful of empty water bottles.

Apparently, she wanted him to walk with her to the pool of water.

"Ok," he agreed and stood up. He noticed he was about two inches taller than her, about the same height that his wife had been. He had a startling flash back of his wife and sort of jerked.

"Are you ok?" Sara asked.

"Yeah…. For a minute there you looked just like my wife and I was shocked." "Really?" she was startled.

"Yeah, you are the same height and build that Sue was, and it just caught me off guard. I'm sorry," he apologized.

"How old was your wife?" she asked

"Well, she was forty-nine when she passed. She really looked good right up to the end," he said. "The chemotherapy made some of her hair fall out, but she was still beautiful."

"I am fifty. I had Taylor when I was still a teenager," Sara remembered. "What happened to your husband?" he asked.

"He was a good man but his family had a history of heart problems. He died a year ago of a stroke. I miss him but I have gotten over it." She looked down.

"Sorry to hear that. It appears we have both lost our life partners." He kept walking toward the eastern island of the atoll as she continued to walk next to him. As they got near the pool of water she turned to him.

"Do you really think I look like your wife?"

"You are pretty close," he said. "But don't worry, I won't make any assumptions about you." He walked over to the pool; it was now only about 5 inches deep. The water was evaporating quickly in the hot temperature. He filled the bottles and they started walking back.

"Does it bother you to have all of these women depending on you?" Sara asked. "Well, to be honest, keeping busy takes my mind off of being with so many beautiful women. I am only human you know," he replied. "Do you think I am beautiful?" she asked curiously.

"Believe me, under any other circumstances I would probably want to ask you out for a date. You are the most attractive and prettiest woman I have met since my wife passed. But that would be totally unacceptable in this situation," he blushed.

"Oh," she replied, also blushing somewhat. Obviously he was attracted to her but was not going to do anything while they were stranded on the island. She figured he knew that if she rejected any advances by him it would cause a lot of unneeded stress between him and the others. She figured that if anyone would have to make the first move, she would have to be the one to initiate it. This gave her a feeling of contentment; at least for now.

He noticed the smile on her face and wondered if she was laughing at his poor attempt to try to be a gentleman. "Come on, we should get back. I have to catch some fish for dinner."

Ron did not catch many fish. He managed two but that would barely feed the women. He went over to the pile of coconuts and carefully de-husked five of them. He shook them to confirm that each had some milk inside. He then opened a small hole in the top of each one using the corkscrew and small knife blade. He then used a plant leaf to plug the holes. He then carried the coconuts over to where the women were sitting in the shade under the makeshift tent he had made of the life raft.

"Today we are having coconuts" he explained to them as he handed each one a coconut.

"Really?" Betty asked. "How do we eat this?"

"Just watch me and I will show you." He pulled the leaf from the remaining coconut and inverted it so it was above his mouth. The milk inside slowly poured into his mouth and he swallowed. It was not bad, he thought. He watched the girls do the same. Only Sylvia missed her mouth and spilled some down her chin. They all started to laugh.

"That tasted ok." Taylor said. "But how do we eat the rest?'

Ron took the coconut from her and walked over to the large rock near the cooking fire. He smashed it on the rock and took the biggest piece and cut the internal coconut fruit into small pieces. He then gave the piece with the cut parts back to Taylor.

"Now you eat the smaller parts," he told her. She took a small piece and chewed it. It was somewhat fibrous but was good. Ron helped the rest of them in a similar manner until everyone had eaten some of the coconuts. He then cooked the meager fish dinner and distributed some to each woman. He was surprised that they all appeared to be satisfied with the food.

CHAPTER 33
DAY 4   1:00 PM

Steve Hariman looked down at Tahiti from the aircraft window. He was Taylor's boyfriend and was supposed to be her fiancé. Just before she left for her trip he had a huge argument with her. He wanted her to do the photo shoot and video in San Diego instead of Tahiti, but she was going to Tahiti and had all of the plans made before she even told him. She thought he would want to explore the tropical paradise with her but it interfered with the plans he had to go on a golfing trip with his buddies. So, they argued. Finally, she threw the engagement ring at him and stormed out of his apartment. She called back the next day and they both said they were sorry but she still was going to Tahiti with her mother. Now she was missing, supposedly lost at sea. He just had to go to Tahiti now; he had no choice with the paparazzi watching his every move. He sat in thought. *'The damn bitch is just too headstrong for her own good.'* Now he would have to look concerned and act like he was mourning her. He did miss her a lot but sometimes she just was too controlling and had to have her way all the time. She had had a string of unsuccessful relationships with a lot of guys that had always ended badly. He sort of knew why now. Still, he thought, he sort of loved her and hoped she would be found. Maybe the experience would change her and she would not be so damned domineering all of the time. He certainly hoped so. He had her ring in his pocket and wanted badly to give it back to her. He would have to act humble and not say something stupid like 'I told you so.'

The plane touched down in Papeete and he got up to leave the plane. There were photographers and paparazzi at the gate taking his picture as he left the gate. A couple of them came up to him and started to ask him questions about Taylor. He really didn't know the status of the search for the survivors so he just pushed past them. Jesus it was hot here. A French policeman was waiting for him and escorted him through the airport to a waiting car. They took him to the French Consulate where he met with the assistant secretary to the governor, a tall man with grey hair in a black suit. "I am so sorry we have to meet under these circumstances," the secretary told him with a thick French accent.

"Is there any word on the search?" Steve asked.

"We are searching the area thoroughly but have found no trace of the aircraft or its passengers. Please be patient and we will let you know at once if we find anything."

"It's been three days. Don't you think something would have been found by now?" Steve acted concerned.

"Believe me; we are doing everything we can." The Frenchman told him. The secretary was under a lot of pressure since the celebrity singer drew a lot of attention. If she was not on the plane there wouldn't be all of the newspapers bothering the consulate all the time for news.

"We have arranged for you to stay at the best Hotel on Papeete until we have rescued the survivors. Our car will take you there." The secretary pointed to the policeman.

"Thanks." Steve said. It looked like he was going to be trapped on this damn hot island for a few days.

CHAPTER 34
DAY 4 2:00 PM

Franklin Carrere was sitting in his hotel room in Bora Bora. He was talking on the phone with his senior production manager, Peter Feldoni.

"Look Pete, it's costing us a fortune to stay here. But the authorities were telling us that they probably would find Taylor in less than 24 hours. I figured we should stay and wait it out, but it has been three days and they haven't been found. They may never be found."

"Look Frank. It would look bad if we pulled out now. The whole country is raising all hell to find Taylor. If we leave now it would look like we are giving up on her. The other artists would not want to deal with us anymore. Why don't you just stay and enjoy the beach?"

"Ok, I understand, but we are going to lose a lot of money if this lasts a week or more."

"I know. But tell the crew that they are on half pay for the forced vacation." Pete sighed.

"Boy, that will go over well. They will want to leave then." Frank was getting angry.

"You have the airplane tickets home, right?"

"Yeah, I do have the tickets."

"Well, if anyone wants to leave, let them buy their own ticket."

"Ok, that could work. But I will lose a lot of crew members when we get back to the states."

"Let me worry about that." Pete replied.

"What about the Tennessee job we had planned for late next week?"

"I will tell them there is a delay."

"What if they decide to hire somebody else?" Frank was getting worried.

"They won't be able to on such short notice. Besides, if you are there to film Taylor when she is rescued, we will get a lot of press exposure. So, keep an eye on the rescue operations."

"Ok. But this is not looking good."

"Just hang in there." Pete hung up.

Frank was about to pull his hair out. Now I got to tell everyone they are on half pay; Jesus, what a mess. He started to pace the floor. His crew was not going to be happy.

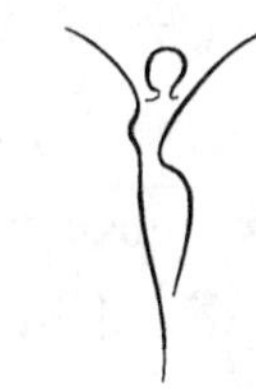

CHAPTER 35
DAY 4   5:00 PM

Ron was in knee-deep water in the area between the beach and the reef. He was not having much luck spear fishing. He had only caught one in two hours. He just barely got a second one but it squirmed off of his spear and left a blood trail. A small four-foot reef shark came over to investigate. He did not have time to retreat so when it came within reach he stabbed at it with the spear. The shark turned to bite him but couldn't because the spear had penetrated its gills. He lifted the shark out of the water and waded back to the beach and threw the beast on the sand. Its tail writhed back and forth trying to regain the water but he grabbed it by the tail and dragged it further up into the trees. He watched and waited and after a while it stopped moving. He had some difficulty in cleaning the shark. The pocket knife was almost inadequate to cut through the sandpaper-like skin, but he finally was able to cut about eight thick fillets from the body and tail and also removed the liver. He remembered reading how shark meat was often sold in restaurants as sailfish since the cuts of meat were so similar. He put the fillets in the cooler and went to the lagoon side of the islet and built a cooking fire. The women were sitting together under the raft watching him. They were still wearing their bathing suits and he had a hard time not leering at them.

"What's for dinner?" Taylor asked, hoping that he had caught something. The previous meal was small in size per person and nobody had been really been able to eat enough to stave off hunger pangs. They appreciated that he was trying to feed them but they were always hungry. They all figured that they weren't going to gain much weight while they were on this atoll.

"Would you believe sailfish steaks?" Ron turned to them, smiling "Please don't make jokes. We are really hungry," Betty replied.

"I will be back in a minute." He grabbed the crude fry pan and went back to the sea side of the islet where he had butchered the shark. He used some of the shark liver to put oil in the pan and walked back to the fire. He opened the cooler and fit two fillets in the pan. He fried the steaks for a few minutes and then forked them on to large plant leaves he had gathered from the bushes. He handed one to Taylor and one to Betty and then went back to get two more fillets. Sara became curious and followed him.

"Just what did you catch?" she asked as he returned to get two more fillets. Then she saw the butchered shark.

"Good food," he said as he loaded two fillets and ran back to the fire. "If you can wait a couple of minutes I will give you one too." Sara sat down with the others and waited. Taylor and Betty were enjoying the steaks, although they had to eat it with their fingers. After frying up the next two fillets he gave one to Sylvia and one to Sara. All of the girls were now enjoying the meal and talking happily to each other on how the 'sailfish' was so delicious. He loaded up two more fillets and proceeded to fry them. Both Taylor and Betty were ready for more, but decided to only split one.

Ron sat down with them and ate one of the fillets. It was not bad and actually tasted good. When he finished his piece he went and got the last two fillets and cooked them, too. He looked at the women. They were all lying down on the sand and were apparently full of fish. He offered the last two fillets to them.

"No, . . . I can't eat anymore, Betty replied. "That sure was tasty though. How did you get a sailfish in these waters?" she asked.

"It wasn't sailfish," Sara interjected. She had followed him and had seen the butchered shark.

"So, what did we just enjoy?" Taylor asked.

Ron turned to her. "Well, Sara is right. It was not sailfish. I caught and killed a shark," he said.

"That was shark?" Betty sat up quickly.

"Yes, . . . but it sure tasted good," Ron replied.

"Wow," Sylvia said. "This is the first time in three days that I'm not hungry." Taylor just looked at him. If she knew that it was shark she probably would not have eaten it. But she had to admit that it did taste good.

"Maybe you can catch some more sharks. This one tasted pretty good." Sara replied, eyeing Ron with a knowing look. Everyone appeared to be somewhat satisfied. The sun was starting to go down now that it was almost evening. Ron collected some wood and grabbed a lit piece of wood from the fire and walked to the ocean side of the islet and re-started the signal fire. Sara went with him and helped carry some wood. Once he had a fairly large fire going , he sat on the sand, watching the ocean waves break on the reef. Sara sat next to him.

"Aren't you scared to be alone with me?" Ron asked.

"No. If you were going to do anything, you would have tried before now." She was pretty sure that she knew Ron by now.

"Don't bet on it," he said looking at her in her bathing suit. "I am only a lonely man sitting next to a very attractive woman that he wants to make love to," he confessed.

"Really," Sara said looking out to sea. "Why don't you then?"

"No, I can't, not here, not like this." He turned and looked out to sea. "When then?" She asked, teasingly.

"If we ever get back to civilization and if you are still interested, well then it might be ok," he replied.

"You are a strange one. I am not sure I have ever met a man like . . . you," she said.

"Well, if we never get rescued, I probably will lose my willpower after a few months and then you better watch out," Ron replied.

"I will look forward to it," she said leaning over and kissing him. He kissed her back but then got up and walked away before it got more intense. He started to clean up the mess he had made of the shark and threw what remained into the water. She got up and walked over to him. "You're serious, aren't you?" she asked.

"Look, I want to make love with you but it just wouldn't be right. What would your daughter think?" Ron was washing his hands in the surf.

"I think she would be happy for me," Sara replied.

"Better not assume anything like that. She is pretty much in charge of her business and is used to having her own way. She would probably think you are too quick to start a personal relationship here on this deserted atoll."

"Well, I guess you may be right, but I am my own person," Sara stated. "I can wait if you can," Ron looked at her.

"Ok. They should find us in a day or two. Nobody is going to give up on finding Taylor."

"I hope you are right," he said as he sat next to the fire. It was now almost totally dark. "You better get back to the girls before they send out a search party."

"Yes. You're right." Sara moved off to return to the raft lean-to on the lagoon side. "Goodnight," she said as she left.

Ron sat there thinking and looking out to sea. *What had just happened?* he wondered. He had almost made love to a woman he barely knew and she seemed very receptive. The pain of losing Sue had not yet diminished for him and he thought that might be why he had turned Sara down. It would still feel like he was betraying his wife. He knew that was probably not the way to be, but he couldn't help it. After 25 years with one woman, he wasn't sure how to be with another woman, at least not yet. He watched the ocean intently. He saw no lights of ships or passing aircraft. *Were they ever going to be found?* He thought. He grew tired and eventually fell asleep.

Chapter 36
Day 4   8:00 PM

Sara returned to the lean-to. Now that the sun was going down, it was getting cooler. Sara went to her suitcase and put on a blouse. Sylvia and Betty were already asleep and Taylor was sitting near the cook fire. It was still burning and the pan with two remaining fillets was sitting on the rock near the fire.

"Where were you?" Taylor asked. "I was about to go looking for you." "I was having a deep conversation with our cook," Sara replied. "That was a good meal," Taylor admitted.

"What do you think of him?" Sara asked.

"He seems nice. He hasn't flirted with anyone yet. I think he may be gay," Taylor joked.

"He is not gay," Sara asserted. "Oh? How do you know?"

"We were almost lovers a few minutes ago," Sara confessed. "That bastard. Did he attack you?" Taylor stood up.

"No. I was the one that approached him. He doesn't want to start anything while we are on this stupid island. I think he is still mourning for his wife," Sara explained. "You approached him? Why?" Taylor hissed trying not to wake up the others. "Because he is possibly the nicest, most honest man I have ever met since your father."

"Mother ! . . . You can't be serious. We have only known him for a couple of days," Taylor whined.

"Listen. You can tell a lot about a person when they are in a stressful situation like we are. He has done nothing except build us a shelter, fought sharks to retrieve our clothes, find water and provide food for us without so much as a thought for himself. You don't meet a man like that very often," Sara looked at her daughter.

"Well, ok but when we get back to civilization I bet he will go to the paparazzi and sell them a lewd story," Taylor replied. "Men always do. I have been betrayed by lovers several times before. You just can't trust them."

"I think this one is different. He as much as said that you would react this way and decided not make love to me," Sara said. "I think he would want your approval before he would be with me."

"Well, that is different, I guess," Taylor held her mother's hand. "Please tell me that you will wait."

"I don't have any choice, according to him," Sara said sadly.

"Well, that is good. Come on, let's get some sleep." They returned to the raft tent and prepared to call it a night. Betty and Sylvia were already snoring.

Chapter 37
Day 4   9:00 PM

The US Navy vessel '*Preble*' was approached by the French Coast Guard boat '*Renégat*'. Captain Patrice Bourne came over to the destroyer in a small launch to compare notes with the Americans. Captain Anderson welcomed him aboard and they went down to the ward room to discuss the search with Lieutenant Olsen joining them. They all sat and scanned a chart of the Tahitian islands. Since the Americans had joined the search, a lot more territory had been covered and the French captain was grateful for the help.

"There is one thing that bothers me," Captain Borne started, "my search aircraft saw a gangster yacht at one of the atolls we searched. When asked about its presence, they replied that they were tourists fishing," he related. "We know for a fact that the man running this boat is a criminal that we have been trying to catch for some time."

"Was the name of the boat "*Pirate*?" Olsen asked.

"Yes. How did you know that? It is an appropriate name for him." Captain Bourne replied.

"Just yesterday I saw that boat at an atoll. My co-pilot said he saw some men carrying machine guns. They radioed us that they were just fishing also, but they did not have any fishing gear out." Olsen explained.

"So, you searched Maupihaa? We already searched that island." "No, this was Manuae, a different island," Olsen replied.

"Really?" Captain Bourne was amazed. "That means he is searching the islands in the area where the charter aircraft went down. His name is Caputo and he is a ruthless gangster. He eliminated his competition in these islands by making them disappear, probably at sea."

"But why would he be helping the search? What's in it for him?" Captain Anderson asked.

"Well, it has been publicly announced that there is a rich celebrity on board of the downed plane. He is not above holding someone like that for ransom," Captain Bourne replied.

"Jesus. That's all we need is to have something like that happen. We must find them first," Anderson stated. "But why is he searching islands instead of the sea areas?"

"He must know something we don't. Maybe he heard a radio transmission that was too weak for us to intercept?" Captain Bourne replied.

"Are there any other islands where the plane could have landed?" Olsen asked. "Well, if they had enough fuel, they could have made it to the Cook Islands.

There are about 20 islands out there, but most are populated. If they went past that there are the Fiji Islands which number about 1500, and most are inhabited. If they had landed on an inhabited island, we would have already heard about it. So that's probably not the case," Captain Bourne explained.

"This isn't getting any easier," Captain Anderson noted.

"What about the satellite photos?" Lieutenant Olsen asked.

"Owens is still working on it, but there are about a thousand photos to scan. It will take a while," Captain Anderson responded.

"That may be our best bet," Olsen said. "Maybe I should help him?" "No, you get your rest. I want you to be fresh to fly tomorrow."

The meeting broke up and Captain Bourne went back to his ship. Captain Anderson went to his cabin and lay down. *I wonder how all this is going to turn out?* he thought to himself. At night the watch was doubled and the ship was slowed to one-third speed with the radar going full blast to scan the ocean surface. Some additional ships were coming to join the search from Pearl Harbor in Hawaii but they were a day or two away. The closest US aircraft carrier was in the Sea of Japan so no carrier aircraft were available.

Ensign Owens was tired from scanning photos all day. His eyes were getting blurry from concentrating on the magnified images of the satellite photos. He finally gave up and went to his cabin. He would get some sleep and then get back to it in the morning. So far he had seen plenty of fishing boats and some pleasure craft but nothing that looked like wreckage. He and the chief had each studied over a hundred photographs but had not seen anything of interest. He knew that the captain would want a report in the morning but he did not have any answers yet.

CHAPTER 38
DAY 5 6:00 AM

Ron had fallen sleep on the sand near the signal fire. He woke up and it was still pre-dawn and the temperature had fallen quite a bit. He walked over to the beach. The tide had gone out and the remains of the shark were exposed on the beach. About twenty crabs were busy attacking the corpse. Ron saw this and looked around for his spear and the cooler. He went back to the lagoon side of the island and grabbed the cooler. All of the women were still fast asleep. He went to the beer bush and grabbed one of the remaining beers. It had condensate on it. He looked at the can. If it cooled off enough at night to generate condensation, it could be a source of water. He grabbed one of the empty water bottles and went into the underbrush. He fashioned a funnel out of a small flexible leaf and then began looking at the large elephant-ear sized leaves. They did have drops of condensation on them. He tilted each leaf so a small amount of water went into the bottle. After about 15 minutes he had filled the bottle with clear, drinkable water. *This is great*, he thought. Then he remembered the crabs. He put the water bottle on a rock near the girls so they would see it and grabbed the cooler. He ran to the sea side of the island and carefully approached the corpse of the shark. A lot of the crabs had left but there still were about eight or nine attacking the corpse. He snuck up and grabbed about four of them before the rest of them retreated into the water. He had placed them in the cooler but they were busy trying to escape, so he closed the lid and walked back to the campsite.

The cook fire from last night was still smoldering so he added some wood and it started up again. Two shark fillets were still sitting in the pan. He took one and ate it cold. It was still pretty good. He opened the beer and enjoyed it with the fish. The women were beginning to stir. Betty got up first and since it had been cold during the night had covered herself with a blouse. She took it off as she stood up but did not notice that her bathing suit top had slipped and he got a full view of her exposed breasts. He pointed this out to her and she turned around and re-adjusted it to cover herself. She was as red as a beet, but he acted as if nothing had happened.

"Want some leftover fish or hot crab for breakfast?" Ron asked. "Sorry about that," Betty murmured as she walked up to him.

Ron had put a crab into the pan after he stunned it by hitting it on a nearby rock. "No problem", he said, smiling.

"I suppose you liked the view?" she asked.

"I won't complain. Nothing I haven't seen before," he said in a low voice. "I was married twenty-five years to a beautiful woman."

"I overheard Sara talking about you last night." Betty took a piece of the shark fillet and started chewing on it. "She said she tried to seduce you and you rejected her."

"Not rejected. More like, let's wait until we are rescued and then see if she was still interested," he replied, not smiling this time.

"You are a strange one," she said sitting next to him. "Would you turn me down too?"

"Well, it would be really difficult, but I think the same logic would apply," he responded, smiling at her.

"Ok. But I am still lost without my Facebook friends. I would like to tell them about you." She wanted opinions from her friends.

"They should find us pretty soon. Then you can get back to your normal life." He was amazed at how the younger people desperately needed their electronic relationships.

"I hope so, she said. "We need to bathe but are afraid to go into the water with the sharks," she complained.

"Well, if you only go in about two feet of depth, and one of you watches for sharks, the other should be able to wash up. Do you have soap and shampoo?"

"Yes, we have some from our suitcases."

"Well, I am going to go over to the other island to get water soon, so you can go ahead and bathe," he replied.

The other women were getting up and came over to the cook fire. Ron handed out crab to them, much to their delight.

"You are getting pretty good at fishing" Sara said smiling at him.

He got up and gathered up the remaining empty water bottles and started to walk to the eastern island. When he got there, he saw that there was only about two inches of water left and the pit diameter was now only about five feet in diameter. He had difficulty in filling the bottles without getting some silt from the bottom of the pit in the bottles. It looked like this water source would probably dry up today. He wondered if there was going to be another tropical storm soon but it was very clear and the sky was an azure blue without any clouds. He thought about how to distill sea water to get fresh water but he had no apparatus to try to do it. *Can't do much with three beer cans and a makeshift frypan*, he thought. He probably could scavenge some metal from the plane, but that would be difficult now that it was totally at the bottom of the lagoon. He sat and thought a while wondering if he could build a raft, and set out on the ocean? It would have to be large to fit all five of them on it. No one would want to be left behind.

He had no ax to cut down palm trees. It would take a while to hack down a palm tree with a pocket knife. Still, it was an idea.

Taylor walked up to Ron, noticing that the pool of water was almost empty. "Looks like we are out of water?" She asked him, her voice a bit shaky. "How will

we survive without water?" She asked.

"We have other sources. Don't worry. Plus, there are always the coconuts." "What do you mean by other sources?" She was bewildered.

"I was able to fill a water bottle from condensate off of the plants," he responded. "Condensation?" she questioned.

"Yeah, if you get up early before dawn, the water in the sea air condenses on the leaves when it gets cooler at night," he explained.

"Oh, I didn't know that." She sat down next to him.

"I didn't realize it until this morning," he explained. He did not add that he could not sleep very well after talking to her mother last night. "Why are you here?" he asked.

"The girls are bathing and I came over here to prevent you from coming back to camp," she explained.

"I hope they are in shallow water and watching out for sharks," he stated.

"Yes, they are following your instructions. But there was another reason I wanted to talk to you," she paused.

"Your mother," he noted.

"Yes. I want you to leave her alone. You barely know each other." She looked at the ground.

"Don't worry. I have no plans to get cozy with any of you. I am still sort of in limbo since my wife died." He looked down also.

"I'm sorry. I didn't mean…." She stammered.

"That's ok. Don't think anything of it," he reassured her. "I still miss my wife and cannot believe she is really gone."

"I hope I end up with a man like you, who doesn't lie about being in love." She stood up. "Most of the men I have been with are just interested in the fame and money I have," she frowned.

"It must be difficult to be so famous. I guess I never realized how hard it must be for you to find someone who is genuine," he replied.

"Yes. It is." She turned away. She stopped a short distance away. "You looked like you were deep in thought when I approached."

"I was thinking of how to build a raft," he replied.

"We already have a raft, don't we?" She was thinking of the inflatable device they were using as a tent.

"Yes, but it is not really big enough for all of us to be on at sea for several days. I am not even sure if we could get it over the reef," he explained.

"You think it would take several days?" she asked.

"I don't know how far off we are from the shipping lanes. I don't know which direction we should go, or maybe rig some sort of a sail and just let the wind take us."

"It might be worth a try," she said hopefully.

"Yes, it might be worth a try. I thought we would be rescued by now," he agreed. "I'm going back to the girls," she said picking up a couple of the full water bottles and walking off.

Ron sat there for a while longer. He would have to see if he could inflate the raft by using his breath. It would probably take a long time but it might work if it still held air. He could fashion a makeshift sail using some of the clothes and tie a palm tree mast to the raft somehow. It might be difficult to get over the reef, but it just might work. By knowing the size of the raft when he tied it to the trees, it appeared to be suitable for eight people space-wise. They would have to take as many water bottles as they had and perhaps some dried fish for food. There were plenty of coconuts he could gather. He would have to fashion some way of putting a shade over part of the raft so the women wouldn't get too sunburned. Since the wind generally comes out of the west, he would hope that it would send them generally back in the direction toward Tahiti. He figured that it could take almost two weeks to do all of the work to inflate and modify the raft. Hopefully the search for them would not be over by then. He noticed that he had a fairly sizeable beard growth from the past five days and it was starting to bother him. He picked up the remaining water bottles and headed back to the campsite. Apparently, the women had finished their bathing and were all back by the raft. He put down the water bottles and started to examine the raft. There was a valve receptacle where the air tank was supposed to inflate the raft. It appeared to have a small check valve so that the air would not rush out when the pressure tank was removed. So, he probably could inflate it with his breath.

It was a large raft, so it would indeed take a while to inflate. Taylor saw him inspecting the raft and came over.

"You think it might work?" she asked.

"It looks possible…but it will take a lot of breath to inflate this thing," he noted. "Well, the girls and I have nothing else to do," she noted.

"Well, let's not start anything yet. I need to plan just how I can fix a sail to this thing," he replied. He needed to think of how to brace the sail without puncturing the raft. He walked over to the stuff he had in his suitcase and grabbed his shaving kit. He continued to walk over to the ocean side of the island. Shaving using salt water could be painful, but he figured it was worth a try. The remains of the shark were all gone as the tide had come back in. He successfully shaved the beard growth and only nicked himself once. It bled a little but seemed to stop fairly quickly. Splashing salt water on his face made it sting but that was tolerable. He figured he should start fishing for lunch so he went back to the campsite and retrieved the cooler and his spear. Maybe he would get lucky and catch enough fish this time. All the time he started thinking of how to brace a sail on the raft. As he put his shaving stuff in his travel bag, he saw a bottle of vitamin C that he typically took with him on trips. He took out the bottle and swallowed a tablet. It would not be good to get scurvy by a strict diet of seafood. Then he thought of the girls and took the vitamins over to them.

"Please take one of these." He said as he handed the bottle to Sara. "What are these?" she asked.

"Vitamin C. It will prevent you from getting sick from eating nothing but fish."

"You mean like scurvy?" Sara knew something about this as she had done a history paper in college on British sailors and how they used lemons and limes to combat scurvy.

"Yes. Please take one each but save the rest for later. "Ok." Sara took the bottle and walked over to the girls.

Ron walked over to the ocean side again and started to look to spear some fish. The fish in this area were getting more wary of him so he moved to a different area. He was really getting tired of eating fish but it was better than being hungry. He fantasized about a big cheeseburger and how good that would taste. Eventually he caught a couple of large fish. He cleaned the two fish and put them in the cooler. He walked back to the lagoon side of the islet. He was surprised to see that the girls were trying to inflate the raft. They were taking turns at blowing air into the inflation valve.

"It's holding air ok," Sara bragged to Ron.

"Well, that's good," he responded. He was amazed that they were so eager to help. They really wanted to get off this island, he thought. They must really be getting tired of eating fish. He needed to figure out how to attach a sail to the raft. They could tie some clothes together to possibly make the sail itself, he thought. The raft was still tied to a couple of the palm trees but it did look as though it was starting to show some inflation.

Chapter 39
Day 5   11:00 AM

Caputo watched through his binoculars as they approached the Motu-One atoll. From this distance he could not make out much detail. This was the last atoll in the Tahiti chain of islands, so he knew the survivors must be here. This was a small atoll with several small islands clustered around a lagoon. There did appear to be an opening of the reef on the chart. He knew this atoll was uninhabited.

"Can you see anything?" Arno asked as he sat next to him and loaded his gun.

"I see nothing yet. I wonder if the plane crash landed in the island growth or landed in the lagoon," Caputo asked himself. If they had landed ok, the aircraft transponder would have been easily picked up by the coast guard, so there was a good chance that the plane was significantly damaged, maybe by the storm. He needed both the plane and the girl celebrity. He really wanted the money that the singer would bring. His customers were expecting a heroin fix and he only kept a small amount in reserve. So, he also needed the drugs.

"The message I got from Teddy was that he had a party of five people, four women and a body guard. So, we gotta think of what to do with the other women," Caputo noted.

"If the women are pretty enough, we could sell them to the Indonesians for the sex trade, or we just have some fun with them and then kill them," Arno suggested. "We obviously have to kill the man."

"That's not a bad idea," Caputo agreed. "But we might have to return the singer alive in order to collect the ransom, I don't like that idea much but if they offer a half million dollars, we could maybe hide out near Fiji for a while afterward."

"Why not ask for a million dollars?" Arno suggested. If she is that famous you probably could get a lot more."

"I like you're thinking," Caputo agreed. He scanned the horizon. No sign of the Coast Guard. They had beaten everyone to the atoll. He just hoped this was the place where the plane landed. Caputo began to think about the hostage. If he let her go she would implicate him in the kidnapping. So, he just might have to kill her after he got the money.

Chapter 40
Day 5   11:30 AM

Captain Anderson was on the bridge of the *Preble*. After four days of searching, they still had not found anything. It was beginning to look like there were no survivors. The Admiral back at Pearl had been getting bombarded for news of the rescue mission but did not have a good answer for the reporters. The Admiral had called him early this morning and wanted some good news. All he could say is that they had not found any sign of wreckage or survivors. The French were not having any better luck either. He was told by the angry Admiral to double his effort. Apparently back in the states this was still a top news story with his ship being identified as the principal search vessel in the area. A news crew that flew into Tahiti had contacted him about landing a photo crew on his ship by helicopter for the duration of the search. Captain Anderson bluntly refused. The helicopter came to his ship anyway but was not given permission to land.

He wasn't about to have a bunch of reporters getting in the way of his crew. As the helicopter tried to land anyway, he had one of the anti-aircraft weapons fire a warning burst. The pilot of the helicopter immediately turned away and headed back toward Tahiti, much to the dismay of the reporters on board. Captain Anderson knew that he was going to get some very bad press for this action, but this was a United States Navy vessel, not a cruise ship. He called for Ensign Owens to come to the bridge.

"Have you found anything yet?"

"No sir. We have scanned the sea up to 300 miles west from Papeete and have not seen anything unusual. There were several freighters and fishing boats but no sign of an amphibian aircraft or wreckage on the water." Owens was very eyesore from looking at enhanced photos for two straight days.

"Well, it's possible that they crashed in the sea and that the aircraft may have sunk." He looked at Owens.

"It is possible sir, but I have not seen any debris or floating bodies either."

"Well, I am thinking that the plane may have flown farther west than we initially thought. So, get back at it." Anderson commanded. "Yes sir." Owens saluted and returned to lower deck. "Man, I do get all the shit jobs," he muttered to himself as he climbed back down to the lower deck.

Chapter 41
Day 5 2:00 PM

Ron had returned to the beach to fish for supper. He had successfully speared a couple of fish. He noticed that at first the fish were not scared of him, but after he had speared one fish, they tended to stay away. So, he again moved further down the beach and had more success. The women all noticed he had shaved and complimented him on looking better. Betty though, liked him better with the beard and told him so. Sara, though, thought he definitely looked better. After cooking the fish for the women and helping himself to one of the fillets, he walked back to the ocean side. He had left his shaving kit near where he had buried Stanley. He sat on the beach and visualized the raft and how to build the sail.

He sat under the palm tree in the shade. The temperature felt like it was in the eighties, but there was a pleasant breeze coming off the ocean. He realized that other than swimming in the ocean, he had not bathed and sort of smelled foul. He looked in the shaving kit and there was a small hotel sized bar of soap. He decided to go skinny dipping. He looked around and none of the women were near so he stripped off his shorts and T-shirt and walked into the water. The soap did not work very well in salt water but he was able to get some lather and washed as best he could in about 4 feet of water. He dipped his head under the surface to watch for sharks but did not see any. The small bar was not very good for washing his hair but he did get some lather. He totally immersed himself to wash off. And then he started to walk back toward the beach. A fin cut the water about twenty feet away and he figured it to be a shark so he rushed to get out of the water. He made it back to the beach before it got to him. He noticed it was about six feet long, much larger than he had seen before on this side of the reef. He got back to his shorts and put them on. He walked back up to the tree line and sat where he was before and started to think about the raft again.

Hidden by the bushes, Sara got up and started to walk back to the campsite. She had watched him bathe, but didn't want to let him to know. He definitely looked better after shaving the beard, she thought, but that wasn't what she was really thinking about.

Chapter 42
Day 5 4:00 PM

Steve Hariman was pacing in his hotel room. He was basically trapped in the room due to all of the paparazzi and reporters who had gathered in Tahiti to cover the disappearance of his fiancée, the missing Taylor Smith. He could not use his social media since it was clogged with requests from Taylor's friends asking him for news. Taylor had been missing for four days now and when he talked to the authorities, they could only tell him that the search was in still in progress. He hated himself for coming to Tahiti. It was the right thing to do but nothing seemed to matter. He did not travel to Bora Bora but stayed in the hotel near the airport in Papeete. He had to leave his phone on in case there was any news of the search. As a result, he kept getting calls from Taylor's friends and he could only tell them that there was no news. God, he hated this. He finally turned off the phone. He really hated this. He could be out on the golfing trip with his buddies. Instead, he had to order room service and stay inside the damn room. He was an actor, had some minor rolls in a couple of films, but he had really only gained celebrity status when he started to date Taylor. Now he was being considered for larger film rolls and had been approached by a couple of directors for upcoming films. If Taylor was dead or presumed so, he would lose his current celebrity status. So even though she was sometimes an insufferable bitch to be with, he put up with her. She had an always "Got to do it my way" attitude. She wasn't even that good in bed, he thought, although he told all of his buddies she was really hot. All he wanted right now was to sneak out of the room and hit the beach, have a couple of drinks and maybe find some female companionship.

He had to be careful in case the reporters saw him. He put his cell phone on the bedside table, and put on a baseball cap and dark glasses. He was wearing a plain T- shirt and shorts with his designer sneakers and peered out the hotel room door. There were some reporters in the hall. He quickly closed the door and walked over to the sliding veranda door to the outside. He was on the second floor but no one was on the balcony below. He slid over the rail and dropped to the first-floor balcony and then jumped over that rail and was on the beach. He was congratulating himself on the maneuver when he saw a bunch of reporters and camera men come out of the hotel entrance. He immediately turned away and bent down to pretend to tie his shoe. They walked by him, not recognizing him. As soon as they were past, he turned and walked in the other direction, toward the pool. The pool bar was almost deserted except for a lone pretty young lady sitting at the bar. He smiled and walked up and sat down beside her and ordered a drink. The young woman was a pretty Oriental in a white mini skirt and a blue halter top. She was nursing her drink, apparently deep in thought about something. He wondered if the girl spoke English. When the bartender brought his drink, he turned to the girl and asked, "Can I buy you a drink?"

"Sure," she said. "My name is Suzy. What's yours?" "I'm Steve." He noted that she was smiling at him.

Chapter 43
Day 5   6:00 PM

Snake Caputo was looking over the Motu-One atoll in his binoculars. His men had searched most of the atoll and found no trace of any aircraft or survivors. They just had to be here. There weren't any more atolls in the Tahiti Island chain. Was it possible that Teddy's plane had enough fuel to get to the Cook Islands? *That would be a nightmare,* he thought. There were about twenty islands in that chain, and only about five were uninhabited. He assumed that they must have crashed on an uninhabited island, otherwise the news would have stories about them being found. He studied the charts again. There simply were no more atolls on the chart.

"I don't understand it." He turned to Arno. "Where in the hell did they land if not here?"

"I don't know." Arno was frustrated. He kept searching each island and not finding any trace of the aircraft or its passengers. "Maybe Chino would know. He was brought up in these islands as a boy." They called Chino over to the bridge. Chino was an island native, somewhat overweight, but fiercely loyal to Caputo since Caputo had pulled him out of the native slums on Tahiti and had made him a rich man. He had a reputation as a stone-cold killer and even Caputo was somewhat scared of him. Chino was happy to work for Caputo since all he had to do was occasionally kill someone and he got paid very well for it.

"Chino, have we missed any islands that you know of?" Snake asked.

"I don't think so." He answered slowly. He was not very bright but he was always careful of what he said. "My brother Arturo used to fish west of here and he told me once that there was another atoll but that it was not on the charts."

"Really." Caputo smiled. Do you think your brother would remember where it was?"

"He might." Chino looked out to the west. "If we head back to Bora Bora, I can ask him."

"Can you call him?" Caputo asked.

"He doesn't use a phone. He fishes on his small outboard and provides fish for the big tourist restaurants on Bora Bora. He used to have a bigger boat and traveled between all of the islands when he was younger. But then he lost it in a bad storm."

"Shit," Caputo turned away, thinking. If they just traveled west it could take forever to find an uncharted island. "Ok. Let's head back to Bora Bora. When we get there, tell your brother that I will buy him a nice big boat if he will guide us to this unknown island."

"Ok." Chino smiled. He would do anything for Caputo. He knew his brother hated him but was also scared of him due to his reputation as a killer.

Chapter 44
Day 5   9:00 PM

Captain Anderson on the USS Preble was becoming frustrated. The search pattern had spread way past Bora Bora and there was still no sign of any wreckage or survivors. He wondered: if the pilot had the aircraft on auto pilot, would the passengers would not have noticed anything wrong until the aircraft started to run out of fuel? They could have possibly crashed near the Cook Islands, hundreds of miles away. Because of this, he had alerted patrols from the Cook Islands to start searching east as he was heading west. The satellite photos had not revealed anything of interest so far. It was a time-consuming job to go through each photo, magnifying each section of the frame, searching for any signs of debris. He was beginning to think that the search was futile and that they would never find any survivors. The Admiral at Pearl was requesting updates about once or twice a day. Apparently the Admiral was under a lot of pressure to provide results, either good or bad.

Typically, a search like this could last almost two weeks before the powers that be decided to give up. One of his helicopters was now down for maintenance which cut his long-range observation capability in half. He was reluctant to keep the one remaining helicopter in constant use in case they needed a water rescue. He was becoming more dependent on the satellite photos but so far they had not revealed anything. The photos were now over two days old. If they showed survivors in the water, the ocean may have moved them with the current. So, the longer they did not find anything on the photos, the less useful they became. He did not dare to request another satellite sweep when he had not fully examined the first set. The French patrol boat was having the same bad luck. Their long-range patrol aircraft had flown constantly for three days and was also down for some maintenance. The aircraft was scheduled to return to its Atlantic station in a day or two anyway. He did not want to admit it but the French did not seem to be all that aggressive in their search. The missing people were all United States citizens after all. The French would return to port to resupply and refuel almost every day. Of course, it was a lot smaller craft and probably did not have a very large fuel tank, he supposed. It was only an inter-island boat, not typically used for large long- range ocean searches. His vessel had somewhat limited supplies also, but he figured he could continue this search for another four to five days before he had to return to Pearl Harbor. Everything seemed to point to not finding any survivors. That was too bad. He had heard of the celebrity singer and was somewhat impressed by her music, but he would not admit that in front of his much younger crew. The boat slowed significantly at night but they kept lookouts and radar on to scan the sea. He figured he would turn in and hopefully they would see something tomorrow.

Olsen was still reviewing the satellite photos. So far he had found nothing but had gone through about two-thirds of the data. Just now he was coming to the far western section of the search area. Maybe he would finally see something important.

CHAPTER 45
DAY 6   5:45 AM

Ron Pritchard woke up from a troubled sleep. He had dreamed that they were stranded on this dreadful island forever and that the women needed medical attention, something he could not provide. In his dream, Sara got sick and died and then Sylvia and then Betty, leaving just Taylor and himself. In the dream they could not figure what was causing everyone to get sick, but it turned out that the fish they were eating was poisonous. Then Taylor got sick and he woke up with a start. It was relatively cool but he was drenched in sweat. *Wow*, he thought to himself. He knew it was only a dream but it really bothered him since he was providing the women with the fish to eat. Then he remembered about the water condensation on the plants and he got up and grabbed a couple of empty water bottles. He walked over to the dense brush and located a bunch of the large leaf plants. It only took him about twenty minutes to fill both water bottles with condensation off of the leaves. By then the sun came over the horizon and the water began to evaporate as it got warmer. *Damn*, he thought, *I won't ever complain about the snow in Cleveland again.* Then he just realized that he might never see Cleveland again. The thought was very disturbing. What if they were trapped here forever? He knew he had to get started to work on the raft idea. It might be their only hope. He hoped he was up to the task.

Ron started to walk back to the campsite when Betty came up to him. She looked worried and concerned.

"What's the matter?" he asked.

"It's Taylor . . . she is having a panic attack," Sara exclaimed. He walked over to where the other women were trying to console Taylor. She was crying and curled up in a fetal position. "We will never get off this place," she screamed. "We are all going to die here," she sobbed. "I am tired of eating fish and being sunburned," she exclaimed.

Ron knelt down next to her. He did not know what to say but figured he had to try. "Taylor, we are going to build a raft and sail out of here," he tried.

"What do you know?" she yelled at him. Tears were running down her face. "I know that we can build a raft and get back home" he replied calmly.

She looked at him. Was he serious?

"You really think that?" she sobbed.

"Yes. All we have to do is inflate the raft and build a sail. I can do that," he said as calmly as he could. She was still sobbing as she turned away. "Leave me alone," she said. He stood up as she appeared to close out everyone, her eyes closed.

"She will be ok in a little while," Sara whispered to him.

"Ok." Ron replied. He was shocked that the Taylor he had read about as being a keen business woman of many talents was acting like a small child. Everyone has their breaking point, he supposed. Being on the island had removed all of her power and she felt very vulnerable. He decided he would walk over to the ocean side and try to catch some breakfast. He was getting tired of fish also but it was the only alternative to being hungry. He had read about breadfruit plants. He wondered what they looked like or if any were on the island. He knew that in Hawaii they had a dish called poi which was a starch substance gained by mashing up the roots of a Hawaiian plant.

It was not very appealing and looked like snot but apparently the native Hawaiians thought it was a delicacy. He wished he had taken a botany class in college. Maybe there was other food here that they did not know about. All he knew was that fish, crabs and coconuts were safe to eat. Coconut milk was a diuretic so he knew that you had to limit your intake of that. He had the cooler and his trusty spear as he reached the beach. Betty came up behind him.

"Is it true what you said about a raft?" she asked. She was wearing a blue bikini that just barely covered her assets.

"Yes. I plan to start it later today," he had a hard time tearing his eyes from her body.

"Can I help?" she asked.

"Well, someone still has to inflate the raft. How is your lung power?" He could tell she had an adequate chest. "We need to build a mast for a sail too."

"OK. I can help with that," she said, not catching his joke. "It is better than just sitting in the shade waiting to be rescued." She appeared to be eager.

"Ok then. I will show you what to do after I catch some breakfast," he smiled at her. She smiled back and he looked into her beautiful eyes again. That was a mistake and he knew his bulging physical reaction to her was noticeable. She noticed it but did not say anything, then turned and ran back to the girls.

CHAPTER 46
DAY 6   8:00 AM

Steve Hariman woke up in a strange bed. His head hurt and he was somewhat exhausted. When he had started the conversation with the pretty Oriental girl, they had hit it off really well. After a few drinks he asked the hotel pool bartender if they served food. The girl spoke up and invited him to her place for dinner. That seemed a lot more attractive so he agreed. It turned out that her apartment was in walking distance of the hotel. Suzy had fixed sort of a fish, rice and vegetable stir fry that turned out to be really good. They had rice wine with the meal and he was soon feeling no pain. One thing led to another and he ended up with her in her bed. He could not remember much but it was definitely the wildest sexual experience of his life. This girl was phenomenal. He got up slowly as she walked into the room totally nude. She grabbed a robe and put it on. She came over and kissed him hard on the lips and told him that the shower was available if he wanted to use it. Then she went back out to the kitchen to make some coffee. He was confused. How the heck did all of this happen? He groggily went into the bathroom and took a hot shower. He went back into the bedroom and found his clothes scattered around the room. He put them on and walked into the kitchen. Suzy wasn't there but another girl was sitting at the kitchen counter. She looked a lot like Suzy but had shorter hair and was dressed in tan blouse and brown slacks.

"Boy, you guys must have really had a good time last night," she said. "I'm Lori, Suzy's sister. I have the other bedroom. When I came in last night I was tempted to join you guys but was too tired from work," she said smiling at him as she drank her coffee.

"You wanted to join us?" he replied. *Wow, that would have been even more intense,* he thought.

"Yeah, a threesome is a lot of fun," she said getting up. "But right now, I have to go to a job interview." She smiled at him as she walked to the apartment door and opened it. Suzy was in the hallway talking to some guy. When Lori left, Suzy came back in with a newspaper.

"How are you doing?" she asked since he looked all worn out.

"I'm alright, I guess" he managed. He looked over to a side table and saw a copy of Celebrity Magazine with his and Taylor's picture on the cover.

"I guess you know who I am," he said pointing to the magazine.

"Yeah, I knew that when you sat next to me in the bar," she said as she poured some coffee into two mugs. "I saw your girlfriend last week when she got on the charter aircraft."

"You saw Taylor?" he perked up.

"Yes, I sold her the ticket to get on the charter plane. She is awful skinny, don't you think?" she replied.

"You knew I was her fiancé and you still seduced me?" he asked.

"Seduce Hell. You were eager to jump on me." She smiled at him, handing him one of the mugs. "Now that the charter plane has disappeared, I have no job," she smirked.

"Well, ok but why now, why me…?" he stuttered.

"Let's just say I was comforting the girl's fiancé since she died in an air crash," she explained.

"We don't know she is dead … yet." he replied.

She opened the paper to show him. The headline was _Lost Plane Not Found_. "You really think she is still alive after missing for a whole week out on the ocean?"

"I don't know," he said, for the first time considering that she really was gone. He suddenly felt her loss, always thinking before that she would be found and they would be reunited. He could feel the acting parts he had been approached for slipping away.

"So, what do you want to do today?" she asked slyly. "We could get a little drunk and go for it again, pointing to the bedroom."

Chapter 47
Day 6   10:00 AM

Ron Pritchard had caught enough fish for brunch and had cooked it for the women, but saved one piece for himself. They were running dangerously short on water, so he had punched holes in a couple of coconuts for the girls to drink from. He had walked over to the eastern island and found that the pool of water had completely dried up. He wondered when the next tropical storm would hit. He remembered from his reading of the Tahitian Islands that these storms typically could occur about once a week at this time of year. It had been almost a week since the storm hit them here when they crashed. He looked expectantly at the sky but it was clear and an azure blue with no clouds. After eating and cleaning up his kitchen utensils, he walked over to the raft to inspect it again. It looked to be intact, with no holes that he could see. The girls had it partially inflated already. He could start measuring it for some structure to hold a sail. If they had a pressure tank, they could inflate the raft easily. The original tank he found had rusted and the air had leaked out over time. He remembered trying to inflate it as the plane was sinking. He liked the idea of the check valve and did not want to damage it. Once they had inflated the raft it would be necessary. It still could be manually opened but it was going to take a while to fully inflate the raft using your breath.

He really needed to figure out the sail and how to attach it to the raft before they inflated it. The long ties that were attached to the sides of the raft gave him an idea of how to fix a crossbar to the mast for the sail. He would have to fabricate some rope to hold everything together but he had seen this done in a castaway movie. It just might work. He started to measure the internal width of the raft with a small stick about a foot long. He then went over to the "Help" sign he had put on the beach a few days earlier and measured a small palm trunk with the same stick. It was just about the size he needed. Sara was watching him.

"You're not going to dismantle your sign are you?" she asked. "Well, no one has seen it yet anyway," he responded.

Sylvia came over to them. "Do we have any water? Taylor and Betty are getting thirsty." Ron went over where he had filled the two bottles with condensation off the plant leaves and gave them to Sylvia and Sara.

"Try not to waste any, it is all the water we have for now. I will get a couple of coconuts and open them," he replied. He then went over to where he had piled some coconuts and opened up a couple. He was successful in drilling a hole in each with the knife and took them over to the girls. Then he started to design the mast and its support in his head. If he had a fair amount of rope he could do it. He would need a palm tree cut to the right width and tie a second palm tree to it as an upright mast and then tie two supports at either side with a long length of rope. Then use some of the tie straps from the mast to secure everything in place. It was a plausible design but he would have to make the rope lengths from strips of bark from some of the local bushes. He had no paper to put his idea on but it looked good in his head. Then he figured he should start thinking about supper. He was getting tired of fish but as he got hungrier, it seemed like a good idea. He grabbed the cooler and his spear and walked over to the ocean side.

CHAPTER 48
DAY 6   1:00 PM

As Caputo's boat entered the harbor at Bora Bora, Caputo was on the watch for the French Coast Guard boat. Luckily, it was not in the harbor. He did not want to tangle with the authorities here. It was sort of an unofficial agreement that they would leave him alone as long as he stayed away from the tourist resorts on Bora Bora. He had Arno arrange getting the boat fueled and he sent Chino ashore to get his brother. If Chino's brother could tell where there was another atoll where Ted's plane had crashed and it was not on the charts, he was sure that he could get the celebrity and his drugs way before the authorities could find the survivors. So, things were turning out ok but he wanted to get going as soon as possible just in case.

Chino was in luck. He caught his brother Arturo just as he was coming back from his morning fishing excursion. Arturo had been somewhat successful and had some fish to sell to the market. He did not make much money fishing, but he was able to make a living at it and support his family. He saw his brother on the dock as he pulled up to it.

"What do you want?" Arturo shouted at Chino. He knew his brother worked with the criminal elements and was shunned by the rest of the family.

"I have a job for you," Chino started.

"Go away. I don't want you here," Arturo replied. "I have to get these fish to market." He gestured at his catch.

"This is small potatoes. I can get you a lot of money," Chino smiled.

"No. I will not work for you or your crooked boss." He started to sort out his catch. "Arturo, please look at me. You don't have to do anything illegal," Chino pleaded. Arturo turned around. "What is it you want?"

"Once you told me that you knew of an uncharted atoll west of here. All you have to do is guide us to it and we will give you a thousand francs," Chino stated in a low voice.

This made Arturo stop and look at his brother. "Why do you want to go there? It is a very small atoll with nothing on it." He was now curious.

"We believe that someone has crashed there and if we find them we get a big reward." Chino knew his brother did not keep up with the news.

"Why not go to the authorities and tell them?" Arturo asked.

"Then we won't get the reward, they will." This logic seemed to make sense to Arturo. He was not as smart as his criminal brother and knew it.

"Ok. I can do this…but I have to get this catch to the market first."

Chino knew it was pointless to argue with his brother over 30 francs worth of fish, so he agreed to accompany him to the market to sell the fish.

It was almost 6:00 PM before Chino and Arturo returned to Caputo's boat. Caputo was very upset that it took so long for Chino to bring his brother back to the boat but he tried to stay calm. When they were aboard, he greeted Arturo and thanked him for agreeing to help him. He gave him a glass of wine to drink and had him sit inside the cabin with him and Chino. Arno was there also.

"Your brother says you know of an island not on the charts." Caputo started. "Yes. I saw it a few years ago when I had a bigger boat and a crew to help me fish." Arturo was enjoying the attention and the glass of wine. "He said you would pay me," he pointed to Chino.

Caputo motioned to Arno. "Pay the man, Arno. Five hundred francs now and another five hundred francs when we get to the atoll."

"Wait. I did not say I would go with you." He looked at the wad of bills in his hand.

Maybe it would be ok, he thought.

"A deal is a deal." Caputo said. Caputo walked over to the chart on a smaller table. "Show me where you think it is."

Arturo got up and looked at the chart. He did not typically use a chart but could see the relationship of the islands he knew. "It is here." He pointed to an area west of Motu One.

Caputo marked the area with an x. It would have been close to the flight path that Teddy would have taken, so it was probably a good choice.

"We leave immediately." Caputo turned and shook Arturo's hand. "Welcome to the crew," he said. Arturo was not happy. He was rich now but he disliked being among these criminals.

"I think we should wait." Randy entered the cabin. "There is another tropical storm coming in from the west." "Shit." Caputo uttered. "At least we can make it to Manupiti before the storm."

CHAPTER 49
DAY 6   2:00 PM

Captain Anderson on the USS Preble walked back and forth on the bridge. He had searched all of the area he had been assigned to without any success in finding the lost plane. Now he was preparing to order the ship back to Pearl Harbor. Apparently there were no survivors of the small plane. He had reported this to the Admiral at Pearl and the Admiral had started to prepare a press release noting that there were no survivors. He hesitated to leave the area without any results of the search but there was no alternative at this point. Typically, a search would last two weeks and the French would keep at it, hoping to find some traces of the lost aircraft. His ship was a US Naval vessel and would need to return to Pearl to resupply since they were nearing their end of their cruise limit. A U.S. nuclear submarine had joined the search but did not have any luck looking five hundred miles west of the Tahitian islands. It would continue searching as it headed west toward the Cook Island chain. The upcoming weather report showed a heavy tropical storm forming in the west and heading toward Tahiti. The submarine could submerge to miss the storm but his ship might be damaged. If he ordered the ship to Pearl now, they just might miss the storm. He did not want to get caught in a typhoon. He gave the order to return to Pearl at flank speed. As the ship turned north he did not think any more about the search, his ship had done their part.

Ensign Owens was just completing the last few frames of the satellite photos when he saw something unusual. He increased the magnification and saw that it was a small atoll on the very edge of the satellite viewing range. As he increased the magnification he saw something that shocked him. On a small portion of the beach, he could make out a sign saying *HELP*. Increasing the magnification, he could just make out two people standing next to it. One appeared to be a man; one was definitely a woman. A few yards away he could just make out a yellow life raft although it was partially hidden in the trees. In the center of the atoll lagoon, something was sticking out of the water. It looked like a small boat but he could not be sure. He copied the views and printed them out to show the captain. He took them up to the bridge. The captain was not there. The Executive Officer Tomas Unger was conning the ship as it was heading north away from Tahiti.

"Where is the captain?" Ensign Owens asked.

"He went down to his cabin. The search is over so we are heading home." the Exec replied.

"I need to see him immediately!" Ensign Owens shouted.

The Executive Officer was somewhat shocked by this outburst but saw that the Ensign had some important information. "Captain come to the Bridge," he called on the intercom.

The captain had just sat down at his desk to write up some reports when he heard the Exec's call. "What the hell is it now?" he asked himself as he got up to go to the bridge.

When he got to the bridge he saw Ensign Owens. "This better be good," he said sternly.

"Sir, look at these satellite photos." Owens implored.

"Let me see." The captain took the photos over to the console and spread them out. "Oh my God!" he exclaimed looking at the photos. "You have found them!" He looked at Owens smiling. "What are the coordinates?" The magnified enlargements did not have the longitude and latitude coordinates that the original photo typically had. Owens gave him the original photo that contained the coordinates. The small atoll was only a small spec on this photo. The captain walked over to his chart of the Tahitian chain. The small atoll was not on the chart and was at the very limit of his chart.

"This island isn't on the chart." The captain noted.

"I am not sure what the thing in the lagoon is sir, maybe a small boat?" Owens replied.

The captain looked intently at the lagoon and saw the thing in the water.

"That is no boat, Ensign. That is a float for a G73 Mallard aircraft! The plane must have crash landed in the lagoon and sank." The captain exclaimed. "This atoll was about a hundred miles west of our search area." The captain turned to the Executive Officer. "Turn us around Tom. We're heading back"

"What about the typhoon?" The Exec asked.

"We will head to Papeete and put in there. We will wait out the storm and then head to this island."

"Should we inform the Admiral?" The Exec asked.

"No, these pictures were taken four days ago. The survivors may have died since then. I don't want to get anyone's hopes up yet. We will inform the French that they should also check out these coordinates based upon our satellite data. They can probably arrive there before we can." The captain hated to let the French get credit for the recovery but time was of the essence for the survivors. Their small atoll was about to get hit by what looked to be a class 5 hurricane. It was doubtful that they could survive without some sort of shelter.

"Ensign." The captain looked at both Olsen and the executive officer. "Yes sir?" Olsen came to attention.

"Keep this to yourself. I don't want someone in the crew phoning home to say we found anybody just yet. I want to confirm that the survivors are still alive."

"Yes, Sir." Olson replied.

CHAPTER 50
DAY 6   4:00 PM

Captain Patrice Bourne on the French Coast Guard cutter 'Renégat' had just put into port on Manupiti to avoid the coming storm when he received a message from the Preble to check out some coordinates that a satellite photo showed might have evidence of the missing aircraft. When he looked at his chart he was puzzled. There was nothing at these coordinates. It must be some debris from the crash. It was outside of his search area but he would investigate it anyway. It was doubtful that the evidence would still be there after the typhoon passed, but he was duty bound to investigate anyway. He closed his chart book and had the crew prepare the boat for the storm. Except for a single sailor, he and his crew would go ashore and stay in a hotel until the storm passed. He and his crew were growing tired of the search anyway and could use a break. The captain stopped as he looked west. Some clouds were already coming into view. He turned to go, thinking favorably of a gourmet meal and a good bottle of wine. He wondered what if there was something at those coordinates. The American ship was at Papeete. If he set out early in the morning he could beat the Americans to that site and possibly be a hero. Although probably unlikely, it was a pleasant thought.

Chapter 51
Day 6   5:00pm

Franklin Carrere was talking on the phone with his senior production manager, Peter Feldoni.

"Pete, we tried to get a camera team on the US Navy boat heading up the search for Taylor, but they would not let us land our helicopter on their boat! And they even had a nice helipad we could have landed on!" he complained.

"Did you ask permission from the Navy?"

"Well…no but we did radio them from the helicopter that we were there to witness the search efforts. You would think that the Navy would want the good press."

"Frank, you have to go through channels. You just can't approach a military vessel without permission. They could think you might be a terrorist and shoot you down. I will call the commanding officer at Pearl Harbor tomorrow and get approval," Pete replied.

"Well . . . We did get camera footage of them shooting at us." "They shot at you?" Pete asked

"It was just a warning shot . . . but we did ask nicely."

"You are damn lucky they didn't splash you into the ocean." Pete was amazed at his subordinate's foolish effort.

"Well, no one is going anywhere tomorrow. I hear that a Pacific typhoon is coming in from the west," Frank announced.

"Crap. It looks like we have lost Taylor Smith as a client for sure."

"Do you want me to start packing up to head home?" Pete asked hopefully.

"No . . . not just yet. Hang in there for a few more days. They still might find her," Pete replied. He really did not want to take a loss on this contract. If Taylor was dead or gone for good, his payment could be held up in probate court for months. Taylor's relatives could claim that they were not going to pay for something that was never completed and he would lose his investment in moving the production company all of the way to Tahiti. He had entered the contract without a down payment from Taylor. She was such a unique customer that he was sure this endeavor would be extremely profitable so when he accepted the contract and did not ask for an up-front payment.

Chapter 52
Day 6   5:30 PM

Ron Pritchard had some luck in fishing today. He had caught another small shark and had cooked 'Swordfish' steaks for the women. Everyone was happy with the meal but they were now out of water. He had drilled holes in some coconuts for everyone so that they at least had something to drink with the meal. Now that the meal was over, he turned to more closely examine their raft-tent. He had finally figured out how he could mount a sail on the raft. He would also make sort of a small cabin on the raft and cover the roof with palm fronds so that the women could stay out of the sun during the day. He figured that he could make a couple of paddles to help them get over the reef. It would have to be a day that the wind blew in from the east. He had noticed that the wind did normally come from the west but occasionally there was a slight east breeze in the evening. He had made all of these plans in his head when a shadow covered him. He looked up. It was getting cloudy and the west wind had increased appreciably. He walked out of the trees and looked west. Dark clouds were approaching. It must be another tropical storm.

He went over to the women who were all laying down in their makeshift beds talking to one another.

"It looks like another storm coming!" he warned them. "Try to get prepared and stay under the raft."

Taylor got up and turned to him. "Is it my imagination or is it getting colder?"

"Yes and it will probably get worse. Better put on some warmer clothing." He hated to say that since they were all wearing sexy bathing suits, but it was a good idea to cover up. The girls started to sort through their suitcases and put on additional clothing. The wind began to really pick up as the dark clouds were almost over the atoll. It was moving in really fast. It started to thunder and rain began to fall. Ron had deliberately placed the raft-tent on a slight hill facing downward so that the water would run away from it in a rainstorm. The women had made a small depression in the middle of the area covered by the raft. They had made makeshift beds on the sand from some of their clothing. He walked around and checked to see if all his raft lashings were secure. Then he climbed under the raft. It was rather crowded with all of them under it

but it was sort of cozy, he thought. The storm really got worse and the wind started to pull on the raft. He told the girls to hold on and they all tried to hold the raft in place. Then it even got worse. The wind ripped the raft in to the air and against the trees it was lashed to. Ron almost got propelled up as he was holding on to the tent. The rain viciously lashed at him and he let go, dropping among the women who were now screaming. They all held on to one another, as the wind and rain ripped at them.

"Keep your heads down." Ron shouted at them as he grabbed Sara's arm. She immediately curled her body up to him, putting her arms around his chest. Everyone was now soaked but the rain did not stop. There was no shelter for them so they just huddled together clasping on to one another. The wind tried to lift the entire group but they managed to somehow keep together, staying in the slight depression. Ron did not know how long they could survive if it got any worse. Then it got worse, much worse.

Chapter 53
Day 6 8:00 PM

Steve Hariman ran to his hotel through the rain showers. He was glad that there were no reporters in the lobby. He walked to the stairs and climbed to the second floor. He was really exhausted after two days of sex with the girl Suzy. All he wanted now was to go to bed and sleep. He had seen the latest newspaper that predicted that the lost plane with his fiancée was now considered to be lost forever. He hoped that wasn't true but now with the typhoon hitting the islands, Taylor's survival was very improbable. When he got to his room, he tried to call the French Consulate for some news, but it was after normal hours and all he got was a leave a message recording. He ordered some food from room service but fell asleep on the couch before it arrived. When it did arrive, he signed for it and tried to eat but kept drifting off to sleep. The storm outside rattled the windows as it increased in intensity but he was deep asleep and did not hear it.

CHAPTER 54
DAY 7   6:00 AM

Caputo was looking out of a window and watching the rain showers. The storm had passed during the night but it was still raining heavily. He had stayed overnight in one of his "Safe" houses run by one of his associates. He wanted to get an early start but had to wait out the rain. They had tied up the boat as best they could to the dock and he was hoping that the boat would survive the storm. He was anxious to get going now that he had a good idea where the plane had crashed. If the Navy kept searching for the survivors, they would eventually discover the hidden atoll. He needed to get there first. He had seen that the French Coast Guard cutter was also in port. His boat was very fast, and he had outrun them before but he was now trapped in port. They could board his boat and confiscate it. He typically relied on one of the French sailors on his payroll to inform him where the Coast Guard cutter was, but that was of no help now. He just had to wait out the storm.

Chapter 55
Day 7   6:30 AM

Ron Pritchard awoke from a troubled sleep. He was drenched and covered with palm fronds which had been torn from the nearby trees. He had passed the night curled up in a spoon configuration with Sara, who had curled up with Taylor who was curled up with Betty who was spooned with Sylvia. Since the high winds had tried to blow them out of the depression, they had held onto each other tightly through the worst of the storm. The depression was now partially full of water. They were all cold during the night and had also clung together for warmth. It was still raining lightly but Ron rolled away from the women and tried to stand up. He got up but was unsteady. It was getting warmer but the rain was continuing. Ron figured that the center of the typhoon had passed to the south of the island since he did not remember experiencing the "eye" of the storm. As it was, the storm had done plenty of damage to the small atoll. Several palm trees were pushed down by the wind. He turned to look at what was left of the life raft. It was severely torn and ripped. It was no longer partially inflated. He sighed; he wouldn't be using this raft to sail away now. The storm had also blown away some of the girl's suitcases and some of their various clothing items were distributed among the bushes. Ron was depressed. He walked over to where he had placed the funeral urn under a bush. Although lying on its side, it was still there and it was still sealed, so he breathed a sigh of relief. It was early but his watch had stopped working (It had water inside the crystal) so he did not know what time it was. Dark clouds were still overhead and covering the horizon. The rain was letting up. Ron walked over to the "HELP" sign he had constructed on the beach. It was obliterated and he was too tired to try to build another. He looked for his suitcase but could not find it or his shaving kit. Now he was really becoming depressed. He sat down on the sand and felt as if they were all doomed to stay on this island forever. He took an inventory of what he still possessed. He still had the small .380 pistol he took off of Teddy in his back pocket. He also had the pocket knife and cigarette lighter he had recovered from Stanley. He went to where they held the campfires. His improvised fry pan was still on the ground near the fire pit but was almost covered with sand. He took it out and cleaned off the sand. At least they could still cook food. Without his shaving kit that had the vial of vitamin C tablets, they were doomed to become sick from scurvy. He wondered how the Natives of these islands had resolved that problem. There had to be an indigenous plant that contained some form of vitamin C, but he had no idea what it was. It finally stopped raining but Ron did not know what to do. For the first time since the crash, he had no idea or plan of action to keep him busy. He knew the women would be waking up soon and looking to him for food but he was just too exhausted to try to do anything. With the clouds overhead he would not be able to see the fish in the water to be able to spear them. So, he just sat there. The feeling of depression was overtaking him and he started to cry.

Sara was the first of the women to wake up. She missed the warmth of the man's body behind her and rolled over. Ron was nowhere to be seen. She was drenched with water but it was starting to warm up.

At least it had stopped raining. She turned to look at the raft that had been their tent. It was ripped in several places. She guessed that Ron could not build a raft to get them off the island now using what was left of the life raft. She was very tired and had only really slept after the powerful wind had let up. She walked around the campsite and finally saw Ron sitting on the sand by the bushes near the water. He was holding his wife's urn but put it back under the bush as Sara approached. She walked over and sat down next to him. He did not acknowledge her presence but had his head down resting on his crossed arms.

"Are you ok?" she asked. "I am sorry," he muttered.

"Sorry for what?" She had not seen him like this before. He looked like he was crying.

"I don't know what to do. We are doomed to stay on this godforsaken island," he whispered. "And I don't know what to do." Ron's voice was unsteady.

"Look . . . we will probably be rescued any time now." She tried to cheer him up. "No . . . If they were going to find us, it would have been before now. We are doomed to stay here and I cannot fix the life raft to make a boat. It is ruined."

"Well then, we will just have to lash some of the palm trees together to make a raft. I see that several of them were pushed over last night." Sara did not want to give up hope and she needed this man who was an engineer not to give up.

Ron thought for a minute. Maybe what she was saying might work if he could make some rope to lash the trees together. He started thinking about it and came out of his depression.

"That just might work," he said, smiling at Sara. "Thanks."

"Good. We need a plan. The girls cannot see you giving up. They will not last long if they see you giving up." Sara implored.

"You think they will go crazy?" he asked.

"They believe in you and need a leader. Taylor would be a leader but she is out of her element here and doesn't know what to do. You must keep it together," Sara stated forcefully.

"Ok. I will try to keep going forward but it is going to be very difficult to build a raft from the palm trees." Ron admitted.

"I knew you would. We all need you right now." She put her arm around him.

"Ok. I think you are a very strong woman," he told her, impressed with her unyielding spirit.

"I need a man who is strong and gentle," she smiled at him.

"Ok. Maybe the water will be clear enough that I can catch some breakfast," he said, standing up. He would do just about anything for this woman now. He hoped she felt the same way for him but he wasn't going to take anything for granted. If she still wanted him after they reached civilization then he would reciprocate.

"Get the rest of them up and try to search for the contents of your suitcases." He implored her. It was still overcast with heavy clouds in the sky but was starting to get brighter.

CHAPTER 56
DAY 7   9:00 AM

Captain Patrice Bourne looked out his window. The storm had passed but it was still raining heavily. The news feed on his hotel TV was showing all sorts of damage to the buildings on Papeete. Here on Manupiti it did not do that much damage. He had slept late and was preparing to go down for breakfast. When the rain had abated he would gather up his crew and head out to the coordinates the US Navy had sent him. He knew that if there was any debris at that location, it would be long gone now. So, he was in no particular rush to get going. The US Navy vessel was still in Papeete so if he left sometime before noon he could easily beat the US Navy to the specified coordinates. He was looking forward to large breakfast and a full day of sailing. One of his sailors had seen Caputo's boat the *'PIRATE'* come into the port. In another time he would have liked to board the criminal's boat and take him prisoner but the search for the survivors (if there were any) was his main concern now. Besides, the inevitable exchange of gunfire could wound some of his men. No, . . . he would wait until he had better odds of capturing the criminal. Besides, he was very hungry and that had to take priority.

CHAPTER 57
DAY 7   9:15 AM

Caputo got his crew back to the boat. The boat had weathered the storm ok. Only one of the mooring lines had come off. The other two lines still held the boat to the dock securely. It was still raining but had diminished to a drizzle. They cast off and headed out of the Manupiti harbor. The Coast Guard cutter was still at its dock. He wanted to get out of the harbor before the Coast Guard cutter became aware of his presence. They had a long trip to take but Caputo was pretty sure that his quarry was at the unnamed atoll island. The fact that it was not on the charts was the probable cause that the authorities had not searched that area. Once his boat was clear of the harbor, he had the captain open it up to maximum safe speed. He made sure that every one of his men had their weapons loaded and ready. Arturo was not happy being with these criminals but he was pretty sure that his brother would protect him. He was not given a weapon but stayed in the cabin of the boat so that he could guide them to the unknown atoll. He told the captain to head west-north-west. It was still very cloudy but the weather report predicted sunshine in the western islands of the Tahitian chain. Going at this speed, Arturo figured they would be near the target island in about five or six hours.

Chapter 58
Day 7   9:30 AM

Captain Anderson on the USS Preble in port was finally getting underway. He now knew the position of the survivors and was going to rush to the site since the storm had passed. His ship was the fastest in the area, capable of 32 knots at flank speed. He should arrive at the small island in a little over 5 hours. He had alerted the medical staff that the survivors may be hurt or suffering from malnutrition. He also had the good helicopter prepare for a fly over of the island prior to the Preble's arrival. With any luck the French will have arrived before him, but he wanted to be ready to provide support for the survivors. He had not yet alerted the Admiral at Pearl Harbor since he did not know if any of the people on the small atoll had survived the bad typhoon last night. As soon as it was confirmed that he had found any of them alive, he would report it. He already knew that if he radioed that they had found something, the word would leak out to the internet and people and reporters would be pressing him for details. He had no patience for that so he maintained radio silence. The crew knew something was up since the ship had increased to flank speed after they had left the port. Instead of heading back to Pearl, they were once again heading due west.

CHAPTER 59
DAY 7   10:00 AM

Captain Patrice Bourne had finished his breakfast and had the crew report to the coast guard cutter. Once everyone was on board, he had the engines start and they headed out of the harbor. He gave his navigator the coordinates to head for. He also noticed that the yacht belonging to Caputo was also missing. Caputo must have feared that the coast guard would confront him and must have left early. It was just as well. He would not have to make up an excuse to his superiors as to why he made no effort to confront the criminal. Captain Bourne was a careful but prudent man. No need to get into a confrontation if it could be avoided. For some reason his ship almost never encountered Caputo. He guessed that a member of his crew was alerting Caputo to their presence. Bourne was ok with that. He was only three years from retirement and did not need any complications in this typical boring duty. They set on their course at normal cruising speed to conserve fuel. He did not expect to find anything at the coordinates the US Navy had transmitted to him, but was duty bound to follow any lead. He had already surmised that there were no survivors from the crashed plane. He sat back and started to think about the pretty waitress that had served him dinner last night. He wondered if she would be interested in a possible intimate meeting. He was a man of influence and wore a fancy uniform. She appeared to be very attentive to his needs. He thought that he would have to return to Manupiti more often.

CHAPTER 60
DAY 7   10:00 AM

Ron Pritchard had found the cooler stuck in some underbrush and his home- made spear was also where he had left it. The women had started to awaken and they were really grumpy so he quickly headed over to the ocean side of the island to fish in the area between the beach and the coral reef. The water was somewhat murky and he stayed in the shallows so a shark would not surprise him. He did not see any large fish but managed to spear two small ones. He also caught a couple of good-sized crabs that did not see him in the cloudy water soon enough to scurry away. It was not much but it would have to do. He headed back to the campsite. He saw Taylor inspecting the remains of the raft.

"I guess this means we can't build a raft." she said to him in a sharp tone. She was frowning and looked very tired.

"No, it just means we have to work harder and make one out of the fallen palm trees," he answered her.

"Really? You can do that?" she asked.

"Yes. That was my initial plan but I did not have enough palm trees to use and had no way to cut them down. But the storm has provided enough for the raft I originally wanted to build," he lied to her.

"Oh, . . . Ok, that makes sense, I guess," she said smiling at him. "Do we have anything to eat? The girls are hungry."

"Oh yes, fish and crab again. I wish I had more variety to offer but the available menu is somewhat limited." He smiled back at her. He needed to put up a confident front so they would not panic as he had earlier in the morning.

"Oh…Crab sounds good." She said as she walked back to the other women. The temperature had risen and it was partly sunny again. So, the women had discarded their wet clothing and were walking around in their skimpy bathing suits. It was all he could do not to stare at them but instead to gather up some wood and kindling to start the cook fire. The women had found some of their clothing items in the bushes but a lot of the contents of their suitcases had simply blown away in the storm. Betty walked up to him as he got the fire started.

"Are we still going to build a raft to get out of here?" she asked in a low tone, obviously concerned that the yellow life raft was somewhat shredded.

"Yep. I have it all planned. You girls will have to help me make rope out of the bark of some of the large bushes. Then we will use that to tie the downed palm trees together. And then we will use what is left of the yellow life raft to build a tent on the wooden one. I figure we can probably start tomorrow and finish it in a few days. Then we paddle out though the opening in the reef and head back to Tahiti," he explained, not taking his attention off building up the cook fire.

"Wow. That sounds really good." Betty turned and ran back to the other women. Ron turned to look at her as she walked away. She was a really sexy woman, and even though she was near the age of one his daughters he was very attracted to her. He shook his head. He had to try to concentrate on nothing except their survival efforts. Sara came walking over and smiled at him.

"You have them convinced that we are leaving this island," she commented.

"I think your idea for a raft was a good one," he said looking up and saw that for the first time she was wearing a bikini. Wow. She was also very sexy. He quickly turned his attention back to cooking the fish.

"Do you like this outfit?" she asked him, turning around so he could see all of it. "Yes, I like it very much. But it does not leave much to the imagination." He

admired her supple figure.

"Maybe you can take it off of me when we get back?" she asked coyly. "Yes. I would really like that." He blushed uncontrollably.

"Good," she replied flirtatiously. She walked back to the others. Jesus, he thought to himself. How can I concentrate on anything with all of these sexy women around? He felt that a part of his anatomy was going to burst out of his pants. Got to try to keep control, he said to himself. He finished cooking the fish and crabs and took them over to the women. They were all very hungry so he only took a small piece of fish for himself. He looked around for the water bottles but could only find two. The rest must have been carried away in the storm. He hoped that the water hole had filled up from all of the rain water. He got up and walked to the eastern island. With only two bottles he would have to make several trips a day to get water. As he had hoped, the volcanic depression was full of water. Based on what they had already experienced, there should be enough water here for about five days. He wondered if they could build a raft in that amount of time. Probably they could not, but they could give it a good effort. He took the bottles back to the women and then wandered off into the dense brush. He found a likely blueish-green leaved bush and used his knife to start to peel off some of the bark. It came off reluctantly but he ended up with about 2 feet of a half-inch strip of bark. He twisted it to make a tight coil and then tied it around a nearby tree trunk. If it dried without becoming brittle, it might be a possible option for rope to tie the logs together. He looked around for other bushes but the only real candidate with enough clear bark between branches was the one with blueish-green leaves. He sat down and tried to think how to build the raft from the palm tree logs so it would stay together.

CHAPTER 61
DAY 7   11:55 AM

Steve Hariman awoke on the couch in his hotel room. He was groggy and still very tired. He saw that the room service tray still had some food on it but it was dried up and cold. He was hungry but could not eat that stuff now. He grabbed the tray and put it outside the door in the hallway. Some reporters were down the hall and started to come toward him. He grabbed the "Do Not Disturb" notice on the door handle and put it on the outside knob and closed the door. He definitely did not want an interview now. His head still hurt from all of the rice wine he had shared with Suzy the day before. That stuff was really nasty he thought. He walked into the small kitchen and saw that there was a coffee maker with some coffee and filters. He loaded a filter with a couple of coffee envelopes and put it in the top. He filled a cup with water and placed it into the device and turned it on. It would be double strong but he needed all of the caffeine he could get at the moment. As the cup filled with coffee, the welcome smell of the liquid got his attention. He took the full cup over to the couch and sat down. His mind was still clouded but he began to wonder what he was doing here anyway. Taylor was obviously gone for good and he was somewhat disappointed but also somewhat relieved anyway. He was tired of having to act nice to her all of the time, especially when she was in one of her bitchy moods. She needed a good spanking he thought. If he was not nice to her, however, she would drop him in a minute. He really liked the attention he got from the press and movie producers when he was with her. He was really getting hungry. The coffee helped but it just wasn't enough.

There was a knock on the door. "Room Service" a voice said through the door. What the heck, he thought. He hadn't ordered anything yet. He reluctantly got up and walked to the door. He hoped it was not some reporter trying to invade his privacy. He opened the door. Suzy was standing there with a bag of good smelling Chinese food and a bottle of Sake. He was stunned. She pushed past him and he shut the door.

"Hello Lover. I figured you might be hungry." she said as she spread the food on the table near the couch.

"How . . . what . . . alright, I am hungry," he managed to say, looking at the food. Suzy was wearing a short white mini skirt, sandals and a green halter top. He was still in his two-day old shirt and shorts. They sat down to eat. He thought it was the best tasting food he had ever had. She poured some Sake into a couple of paper cups and it really went good with the food. After the meal he sat back on the couch and promptly went to sleep. Suzy looked at him disappointedly but went over and turned on the TV. She sat next to him and watched a movie on the movie channel. Later, when he woke up and looked around, he saw that she was still here. She saw him wake up and stood in front of him.

"Have a good nap?" she said.

"Yes, I suppose so," he said, about to ask her to leave. At that point she slid out of the skirt. She had no underpants on. She bent down to kiss him.

"Oh my God." He muttered as she bent down and removed his shorts.

Chapter 62
Day 7   1:00 pm.

Ron Pritchard walked over to the tree to which he had tied the strip of bark. It had dried and was somewhat flexible and tough, but not brittle. He had to use his knife to cut it off of the tree. This material just might work to tie the raft together. He had one more test to make. He walked to the beach and submerged the piece of bark under water, held down on one end by a rock. If the material did not dissolve apart in sea water then it would be ok to use. He was starting to feel better about building a raft. He walked over to the campsite. The women were sitting in the shade and talking among themselves. He looked around and he spotted quite a few downed palm trees. He went over to one and tried to pick it up. It was too heavy for one person. He then tried to drag it across the sand. He did make some progress but after he had moved it about 20 feet, he had to drop it. If this was going to be successful, he was going to have to harness some girl power to help move the logs together. The sun was directly overhead and very intense. This was not the time to get them out of the shade to do grunt work. He would wait until the evening when the sun had moved to the horizon to get them to do this work. He decided to find a shady spot and take a nap. As he fell asleep he was thinking about the buoyancy of the palm trees. He would have to test one in the lagoon to see how it would float.

Chapter 63
Day 7 2:00 PM

The day had become sunny with few white clouds on the horizon, and the *PIRATE* moved through the now calm water swiftly. Arturo looked at the horizon with the binoculars. They were getting close to where he remembered the unnamed atoll was. He remembered it being a very small atoll with nothing remarkable about it. It had a small lagoon that he had fished in several years ago. The fishing was not that good so he never returned. The atoll was really desolate with nothing there of any value. He wondered why Caputo wanted to go there. Still, the money was good so he had agreed to guide them. The highest point of the small island was only about 40 feet above sea level so it was hard to see from a distance. That is probably why it was never put on a chart. He had only discovered it by accident. Caputo watched with interest as Arturo guided the boat. The man was definitely an asset and he could become a welcome addition to the crew. He figured that Arturo probably would not want to join up, however, since all he ever talked about was fishing. Arturo's brother Chino was a stone-cold killer and had eliminated several problems for Caputo. Even Caputo was amazed that killing people did not seem to bother Chino. He was quite good at it and never seemed to fail at eliminating whoever Caputo asked him to. He was apparently extremely loyal and never questioned Caputo on anything. The rest of the crew were terrified of him and did not turn their backs on him. Even Arno, his second in command, had quiet respect for Chino.

Chapter 64
Day 7   2:30 PM

Ron woke up from his short nap and saw Taylor walking towards him with two empty water bottles.

"Is there water at the water hole from the storm?" she asked him. She was still wearing a blue bikini but had a loose, unbuttoned white blouse on. She had found one of the broad straw hats and had that on also, protecting her from the sun.

"Yes. I got some water there earlier this morning. He got up to walk with her to the east island. "Did you guys find much of your clothing? The storm really hit us hard last night."

"We found some of it. Enough to keep us decent for a while, I guess." She did not have any sandals on but was walking barefoot. The sand was hot so she walked along in the water that almost covered the sand path to the eastern island. She looked pensive. "Do you really think we can build a raft and leave?" she asked.

"Definitely. Now that we have all of these downed palm trees, it will be a simple matter to move them to the lagoon and lash them together. I have found some bush bark that we can strip off and use as rope. Then rig a small sail and a tent using what is left of the yellow life raft and we are good to go." He had it all planned in his head.

"How long will it take us to build it?" She asked.

"That depends on how long it takes to prepare the rope. Maybe it will take a few days."

"What will we use as food and water?" She was becoming interested.

"Well, we have plenty of coconuts and I will catch some fish and cook it before we leave. Once we are out of here, we will probably be found by a passing freighter in a day or two." He was starting to feel confident.

"It sounds like you believe we can do it," she replied. "Got to have a plan," he responded.

They got to the island and climbed though the underbrush. There was almost a worn path to the water hole now. They got to the depression and filled the water bottles. He then walked over to the ocean side looking north. She followed him, curious. He sat on the sand and she sat next to him. They looked at the broad expanse of the blue ocean stretching out to the Horizon. Some small white clouds were on the horizon. There was a slight sea breeze, but the waves crashing into the surrounding reef were very slight. He turned to her.

"I have to tell you, . . . I think I am falling for your mother. She is very much like what my wife was. And we may want to get together after all of this is over," he confessed.

"I sort of got that impression from her, too." Taylor admitted. "I think you are an honorable man and won't hurt her."

"I wanted you to know . . . in case you object, I will not pursue her." He looked her in the eye.

"No, I don't object. She has not looked this happy since my father passed."

"Ok. I just want you to know that I won't be of any financial burden on you. I have a very healthy stock portfolio and have a good job as an engineer."

She laughed. "That is just what I expected from you. You seem to be strongly self-sufficient."

They sat there for a while, enjoying the cool breeze off the ocean.

Chapter 65
Day 7   3:00 PM

Caputo looked at the picture. It was a photo of Taylor Smith that he had printed off the internet. She was very pretty. And she was outrageously rich. He was thinking of asking a cool million dollars for her return. He was also thinking about the body guard. They would probably have to kill him but that was no big deal. He had his men all armed with Uzi machine guns. He had his full team with him. Arno, Chino, Uri, Huwala and Randy, the boat driver, were all armed and ready to go. Arturo was along but was not yet part of the team. If they had to kill the body guard he hoped that he could depend on Arturo's silence on the matter. He would hate to ask Chino to kill his brother.

The sea was calm with a slight swell. That made it easier for the boat to move swiftly. There were some light white clouds on the horizon but the weather report called for clear conditions for the next two days without any storms. Caputo figured he could nab the singer and make it to his hideout without anyone noticing. Then he would shock the world by announcing that he had her and demand the ransom. He was not quite sure how he would arrange the payment but he was thinking a deposit into one of his off shore accounts would work. After it was deposited he would quickly split it and transfer it into several other accounts that the authorities could not trace. It would be easy to release her. He would put her in a lifeboat and then cruise away. When he was far enough away he would report her position. He of course, could do other options with her, such as tie a cement block to her ankles and drop her in the ocean. That was probably a better solution without any way for her to ID him to the authorities. Yes. That might be a better solution. His men could have their way with her before doing that of course. It was a pity that the pretty singer would have to disappear but he always was a cautious man. He needed to keep her alive long enough to get the money, would probably have to show photographs of her with a current newspaper.

"I think I see something!" Randy called from the bridge.

Caputo ran to the side rail and looked across the water. Far off he could see a small flat island. It was an island that was not found on any chart. He smiled widely.

"Arturo! Is this the island?" Caputo shouted.

Arturo walked over to Caputo. "Yes, I think this is it. If you go to the western side of it there is an opening in the reef due to a sudden drop off of deep water." Your boat should be able to enter the lagoon there." Caputo pointed to the western end of the small island. "The lagoon is not that deep, maybe 25 feet or so. It was terrible for fishing."

"OK. Let's head for the west end. Keep our speed slow. I want to quietly surprise anyone on the island. You guys load your weapons," he ordered the crew. Arturo was confused as to why they were preparing to attack if this was a rescue, but he had done his part and fully expected to get the other 500 francs. "You got my money?" he asked quietly. Caputo looked at him. "Yes, of course. Just wait until we get what we came for," he growled. Arturo stepped back. Now was probably the wrong time to ask. They waited as the boat rounded the island slowly and they could see the opening into the lagoon. As they entered the lagoon slowly, Caputo could see some signs of a campsite. And then he saw three women sitting in the shade. One of them saw him and stood up waving her hands. All of them rushed to the beach. They were all wearing bikinis. Caputo would have to control his men until he had secured the singer and found his drugs he thought.

CHAPTER 66
DAY 7   3:20 PM

Betty was sitting with Sara and Sylvia, discussing Ron's plans for the raft and what they could do to help him build it. Betty looked up as the 56-foot yacht slowly moved into the lagoon. At first she could not believe her eyes. Then she jumped up and yelled "We're saved." And then she started to run toward the beach facing the lagoon. Sara and Sylvia got up and turned to look.

"Oh my god. It's a ship," Sylvia screamed as she also started to run toward the beach.

"Thank god," Sara muttered as she turned to walk toward the beach. It was a large yacht, she thought. She joined the other girls at the edge of the beach. Sara could see several men on the boat and she realized that she was wearing a blue string bikini, not the most conservative covering. She thought about going back and getting a blouse but was too interested in what was happening to move away. The yacht was about 50 yards from the shore and she could see that they were lowering a small motor boat in the water. Four men climbed into the small boat and they turned it toward the shore as they started the motor. Sara was watching with great interest until she saw that two of the men were carrying machine guns. Why would a rescue party be carrying machine guns?

"Sylvia; Look, they have guns!" Sara exclaimed.

Betty and Sylvia began to back away from the water. "Why do they have guns?" Betty exclaimed. Sylvia looked at Sara; "They don't look very friendly. We may be in trouble." Sylvia started back to the camp to find something to cover her bathing suit. Sara and Betty just stood frozen in place. There was no place to go, no place to hide. Sara figured she would tough it out and be the spokesperson for their group.

The small boat landed on the beach. Two of the men got out and pulled up on the sand so their leader could step out onto the sand. He was somewhat shorter and fatter but moved with authority. Sara could tell he was the leader since the other men only moved to follow him. Caputo approached Sara.

"Are you the lost party from Teddy's aircraft?" he asked her. He could tell that she was not the singer he was looking for but she was an older woman and apparently was in charge.

"Yes. Have you come to save us?" Sara replied. These men looked rugged and tough and were pointing their guns at her. She did not like it. "Why do you have these guns?" she asked.

The short fat man laughed. "Yes, we are here to rescue you." He could not stop laughing. "Chino, go to the top of that hill and keep a look out." Caputo was nothing if not cautious. He knew that others were looking for the survivors and he did not want any surprises. Chino trudged off toward the top of island, the Uzi in his hands.

"Now tell me woman, where is the singer?" "You mean my daughter, Taylor?" she asked. "Yes. Where is she?"

"She went off to fill our water bottles at the other island. She should be back soon." Sara stopped. She was giving out too much information.

"Where is the bodyguard?" Caputo asked, looking up and down the beach.

"You mean Stanley? He was killed by a shark when we landed . . ." Betty blurted out, not knowing if she should share that with these men. The other two men were leering at her and she tried to cover herself better with the unbuttoned blouse she had on.

"So, the bodyguard is dead?" Caputo asked Sara.

"Yes. He was attacked in the water after the plane crashed." Sara looked down at the sand.

"Good. That makes things simpler. And Teddy? Is he dead also?"

"The pilot had a heart attack and we crashed into the lagoon." Sara pointed to the yacht.

"OK. Now, . . . Where are my drugs?" He asked forcefully. "Drugs? What drugs?" Sara was puzzled.

"You didn't see the drugs?" Caputo was wondering, maybe the drugs were still on the plane. "Where is the plane? Did it sink in the Lagoon?"

"Yes. Shortly after we hit the water it began to sink and we had to swim to this island," Sara explained.

Caputo turned to the tallest man. "Arno, get your diving equipment and see if the drugs are still on the plane." Arno gave his Uzi to Caputo and turned and got his scuba tank from the boat. He got his gear on and waded out into the water.

Sara looked at Arno and said "There are big sharks in the water" "Arno can take care of himself, don't worry," Caputo replied.

That just left the short fat man with the other man who held an Uzi pointed at them.

Caputo looked at the women closer. They did not look like they had been starved for a whole week. They looked to be in good condition. He wondered where they got the food.

"You have been here a week. What did you eat?" Caputo asked. "We had some fish and crabs that we cooked." Betty answered. "That is remarkable. How did you catch the fish?"

"Ron caught…." Betty stopped. She somehow knew that Sara had deliberately not mentioned Ron and now she had ruined it.

"Who is this Ron?" Caputo shouted at Sara.

Sara shrank away from his tone. "He…he is another passenger that was on the plane." Sara barely whispered.

"So where is this Ron guy?" Caputo asked in a more moderate tone.

"He went with Taylor to get the drinking water. There is a place on the eastern island where there is water."

Caputo took Arno's Uzi and pointed it in the air and fired off a burst of automatic fire. The women retreated with the loud sound of the gun. Caputo turned to the women. "That should bring them back here," Caputo smiled. "Move back into the trees now." he ordered the women.

CHAPTER 67
DAY 7   3:30 PM

Captain Patrice Bourne was on his bridge looking through his binoculars. He turned to his navigator. "How far are we from those coordinates I gave you?" he asked.

"It looks like we are about 35 miles from the position. We should be there in a few minutes, Mon Capitan," the navigator responded.

Captain Bourne only had a crew of eight today. Two of his men had called in sick this morning. Probably had drunk too much wine last night in port, he thought. Still, he only really required a crew of six to run the coast guard cutter. It was a nice clear day and the boat had made good speed this morning. He had cut back to a slower speed this afternoon to conserve fuel. He did not think there was any rush anyway. There would be no survivors after a week at sea he thought.

CHAPTER 68
DAY SEVEN   3:45 PM

Ron was just about to get up when he heard the automatic weapon fire. He turned to Taylor who had been sitting next to him on the beach.

"What was that?" she asked.

"Sounded like gunfire to me." He replied. "We better get back there quick." "Maybe we are rescued?" she said, dropping one of the water bottles but not

stopping to pick it up since she was running behind Ron who was making it to the lagoon side of the atoll. As he broke through the underbrush he saw the big white yacht. As he stopped short Taylor almost ran into him.

"Boy does that ever look beautiful?" he noted with a big smile. "It looks like we are going home."

Taylor was out of breath so she did not say anything, but she also smiled. They ran along the narrow beach between the two islands until they got within sight of their camp. Ron saw two men with the women. He stopped running since he saw that both of the men appeared to have machine guns pointed at the women. What the heck was going on? He wondered.

"Why do they have guns?" Taylor asked innocently.

"I don't know but we are about to find out." Ron reluctantly walked up to the group.

A short fat man wearing khaki pants and a tan shirt turned toward him. "What is your name?" he asked Ron.

"I am Ron Prichard." Ron replied looking at the other man with the Uzi. "Should I kill him now, Boss?" Uri asked, lining up the weapon on Ron.

"No, not yet. We have all day to figure out what is going on here." Caputo moved

his hand away from Ron. He was much more interested in the pretty girl singer who was standing next to Ron.

"So, you are this Taylor Smith girl?" he asked her. "Yes..." Taylor said with an obviously nervous voice.

"You are the one everyone is looking for. And now you are mine, all mine." Caputo stated. "Do you think they will pay a million dollars to return you?" he asked her.

"Is that what this is about?" Sara asked from the side.

Caputo turned towards Sara. "I am a business man. And my business is making money. Anyone who stands in my way gets eliminated." He turned back to Taylor. "I am going to take you for a little boat ride, my girl." He actually drooled a bit when he said it to Taylor. Ron looked over at the yacht. It was a big one, probably a little over 50 feet in length he thought. He turned back to Caputo. He had to do something to stop all of this, but could not think of anything.

"So, you had a pretty good gig here with four naked women, huh?" He looked at Ron slyly.

"It wasn't like that; he was a perfect gentleman," Sara said looking at Caputo with hate in her eyes. This evil man intended to hold her daughter for ransom. She immediately despised him.

"Well, well, well. Looks like you missed your chance buddy. These are prime women for sex." Caputo thought for a minute. Maybe he could hold the girl for ransom and sell the rest of them to a sex trader he knew.

"Are you gonna let us have the other women?" Uri asked Caputo.

"Hold on. We can sell them a sex slaves to that guy in Malaysia. These pretties would bring top dollar, except for the old one. You guys can do what you want with her." Caputo smiled.

"That's my mother. You can't do that." Taylor shouted at Caputo.

"Caputo turned and pointed the Uzi at Ron. "You want me to start the killing now?" he shouted back.

"No, please. Don't kill anyone," Taylor pleaded.

"Well, I have no use for this guy as he cocked the weapon and pointed it at Ron. Just then Arno surfaced about midway between the yacht and the beach. He shouted at Caputo "The drugs aren't on the plane. They must have found the package."

Caputo turned to Ron. "You found my drugs?"

"Yeah, I found your drugs." Ron hissed. He did not want to say it, but he figured they might let him live a bit longer.

Caputo walked closer to Ron, not lowering the weapon. "OK, wise guy, where are my drugs?"

"I hid the bag where no one will ever find it." Ron stated.

"You will take us where you hid it." Caputo said with no emotion.

"Why should I, if you are going to kill me anyway?" Ron was thinking about the small .380 pistol in his back pocket that he had taken off of Ted's body. Maybe he could pull it out and use it when they were not looking.

Caputo pointed his pistol at Sara. "Where do you want me to shoot her first; the right knee or the left one?"

Ron was horrified. "All right…all right. I will take you to the drugs. Just don't hurt the ladies." Ron knew he was defeated. But as long as he had the small pistol, he had a slight chance.

Sara looked at him "Don't give in to them," she whispered.

"He doesn't have much choice." Caputo said to her. We are the ones in charge here. We are the ones with the guns." He smiled and turned to Arno.

"Arno. Take off the gear. Make him show you where the drugs are." He blinked at Arno. Arno understood that once he had the drugs he could kill the man. Caputo handed Arno his Uzi back and whispered to him "use your knife." It would be silent and would not upset the women. Arno dropped his gear, nodded to Caputo and walked over to Ron, turned him around and pushed him forward holding the Uzi at Ron's back. "Show me now," Arno said in a low voice.

CHAPTER 69
DAY 7   4:00 PM

Captain Bourne could not believe his eyes. He could see a flat low island ahead that matched the coordinates the US Navy had provided. It was not on any of his charts for this area. As they approached closer, he could see the top of what appeared to be the mast of a ship inside the island.

"This must be an atoll. Let's try to find an entrance to the inner lagoon." He commanded. Maybe this is why the US Navy gave him these coordinates. Their satellite must have taken a picture of this remote area. If the plane had landed here, there could be some survivors. But what of the mast he saw? As they rounded the island he could see a passage into the lagoon. Through his binoculars he could see the yacht *'PIRATE'*. It appeared that Caputo had beaten them to the survivors. He would have to confront the criminal now. Maybe a show of force would convince Caputo that it was useless to resist. Or at least he hoped. He stopped his boat and announced battle stations to his crew. They had one major gun; a .30 caliber browning machine gun mounted on the front of the boat. Ha had a man unsheathe the cover of the gun and attach a box magazine with live rounds, and prime the weapon. The only other weapons on board were five old bolt-action rifles. He had his .38 caliber revolver also. But he was short of men. One man had to be in the engine spaces, and the navigator had to drive the boat. That only left four men to use the rifles. He unlocked the case containing the rifles and handed them out with ten rounds each. If they needed more than that he figured he would be in trouble. He had the four riflemen line up on the cupola behind the bridge. He remained on the bridge. He would try to bluff Caputo into thinking he had more firepower. He told them not to fire unless he gave the order. He made sure the man on the deck machine gun heard him also.

Chapter 70
Day 7   4:00 PM

Caputo was looking at the singer. She was very pretty but she was too famous to be sold as a sex slave. He would have to kill her after he collected the ransom money. It was a pity he thought. At least his men would have their way with her first. After they were done with her she wouldn't want to live anyway. He himself was not interested in carnal-rape pleasures; he was only interested in the money. He had his wife back at home and was true to her. Just then Chino came running down the hill.

"The Coast Guard cutter is coming!" he shouted to Caputo.

"What? How did they get here?" Caputo was stunned. These women were stranded here a whole week and a half hour after he finds them the Coast Guard appears suddenly? What were the odds?

"Let's get back to the yacht," he said to Chino. He turned to Uri. "You stay and watch them. Don't shoot the singer no matter what. If she tries anything, shoot the mother first."

"Ok," Uri grunted as he pointed the Uzi at the women. They stayed sitting down in the shade where he told them to. Sara had heard them talk about the Coast Guard. Apparently the Coast Guard would fight the pirates and they would be rescued. She whispered to the girls: "The Coast Guard will save us." Taylor began to have some hope again.

Caputo and Chino pushed off in the small boat and tied up against the yacht while the Coast Guard boat paused outside of the lagoon. Caputo told Randy to move the boat further into the lagoon and turn it so it was perpendicular to the lagoon opening. Then he got Chino and Huwala down in the cabin and gave them each an M72 LAWS rocket. Arturo was in the cabin also and he looked at the military grade hardware and was amazed. "What are you guys going to do?" he asked.

"You just stay down here and keep quiet if you want to get your money." Caputo shouted at him. He and the others went topside and hid below the railing facing the opening of the lagoon. Both criminals knew how to use the small bazookas and prepared them to fire. Caputo drew his pistol and stood where the captain of the Coast Guard could see him.

"Don't fire until I tell you. One of you take out the machine gunner and the other aim for the riflemen," he ordered in a low voice. Randy had an AR-15 and was also hidden on the bridge cabin of the yacht.

Captain Bourne had his vessel enter the lagoon slowly. He did not trust Caputo and wondered why he was here. As he entered the lagoon he had his navigator turn broadside to the yacht so Caputo could see the machine gun and four riflemen aiming at him.

"What are you doing here?" Bourne called across the water, pulling out his revolver.

"Captain Bourne. Do you want to split a million dollars?" Caputo shouted back. He had no intention of actually splitting the ransom money but it was always best to appear to negotiate to get an advantage.

"What do you mean?" Bourne replied. He was immediately interested in some sort of cash deal where he got a lot of money.

"We hold the singer for ransom and split the take 50-50," Caputo shouted back.

Bourne stopped to think. That was a lot of money. But he would have to split it with the crew to keep them quiet. That would lower the amount he got. Also, the singer was a high profile celebrity. She was famous and if it ever got out that he helped hold her for ransom he would be hanged. He just could not do it this time.

"How about we let you leave peacefully and we rescue the girl." Bourne still wanted to avoid a confrontation if possible.

CHAPTER 71
DAY 7   4:15 PM

Captain Anderson on the US Preble was now about thirty miles from the island.

He called his ace helicopter pilot, Lieutenant Olsen to the bridge.

"Olsen, I want you to fly out to the island ahead and see if there are any survivors. If they are still alive, they may be in pretty bad shape so take some water and food with you. Have the cook make up some sandwiches. If they are still alive, let them know that we will be there in about 20 minutes or so. Got that?"

Olsen stood at attention and replied, "Yes, Sir" with a big smile. He was a big fan of the famous singer and it looked like he would finally get a chance to meet her. He turned and headed to the galley.

Captain Anderson wondered if the French had gotten there already. He knew they had left from Manupiti which was a lot closer to the island then he had been at Papeete this morning. He hoped that the survivors were still alive, but it was doubtful after a week of starvation and possible dehydration. It probably was not possible to survive yesterday's typhoon anyway. Even if one or two of them were still alive it would be a miracle. He was hoping for the miracle but he was a pragmatist.

Chapter 72
Day 7   4:20 PM

Ron walked up the hill where he had buried Stanley and the drugs. The big guy pushing him was about six foot six and must weigh about 280 pounds. He was only wearing black diving shorts and looked very well-muscled. He looked to be in top shape and had at least an 80 pound advantage on Ron. The man had a mean look to him also. They got to the top of the hill. Ron turned to him.

"Want me to show you where to dig?" Ron asked. The bigger man lowered the Uzi and walked up to him about a foot away. He side kicked Ron in the face with his right foot. Ron went down, seeing stars and sort of blacked out. He did not even see the kick coming, it was so quick.

"I got a black belt in Karate." Arno gloated over the fallen figure. "You dig. And be quick about it." He put the Uzi strap around his neck and shoulder so that it was on his back. He then took out his razor sharp diving knife from the sheath on his hip.

Ron slowly came up to a sitting position. He was puzzled. Why did the big guy do that? Was he just showing off or did he get off on picking on smaller guys? He struggled to his knees and held up his right hand as if asking for mercy. His chin was sore.

"Ok . . . Ok. I'll dig." He looked around for the piece of driftwood he had used for a shovel before. He had left it as a marker for Stan's grave but the storm must have blown it away. So, he started to dig in the general area with his hands. He glanced up at Arno and saw the big knife in his hand. Ron knew what the knife was for. He knew that he did not have much time left. The small pistol was still in his back pocket but he would never have enough time to use it.

Chapter 73
Day 7   4:25 PM

Captain Bourne had offered to let the criminal Caputo leave peacefully. Caputo appeared to be considering it.

"You promise not to shoot us if we leave?" Caputo shouted to Bourne.

"We promise," Bourne shouted back, somewhat relieved that Caputo was backing down.

"Have your men lower their weapons then." Caputo sounded beaten.

Bourne ordered his men to stand down. Caputo saw this and dived to the deck. "Now." He shouted at his men. Both Chino and Huwala stood up and fired their LAWS rockets at the Coast Guard boat. Chino's shot took out the four riflemen and started a major fire. Huwala's shot was off and hit the Coast Guard cutter near the water line under the Browning machine gun position. The explosion knocked that sailor to the deck under the gun and as he tried to get up Randy shot him several times with the AR-15. While the two loud explosions caught Bourne somewhat off guard, he recovered enough to shoot Huwala in the forehead with his pistol. The Coast Guard cutter was definitely on fire and sinking rapidly. Chino and Caputo now used their Uzis to spray the cutter with several rounds. Bourne ducked this fire and realized his ship was done for so he jumped overboard on the opposite side of the cutter. With no more threat from the Coast Guard cutter which was now on fire and listing heavily to port, Caputo stopped firing. Black smoke was billowing up above the stricken vessel.

Just about at that time, Caputo heard a helicopter coming. He looked up and saw a helicopter.

"Now what?" he said, exasperated. He turned and started to fire his Uzi at the helicopter. Randy and Chino started to do the same.

Lieutenant Olsen had just seen the island and started to enter the lagoon when he saw the explosions on the French coast guard cutter. He paused, but then banked to the side to avoid the ground fire. He radioed the ship.

"Alert! . . . there are two ships in the harbor…one is on fire and the other is attacking me. I am receiving ground fire and turning away."

CHAPTER 74
DAY 7   4:20 PM

Ron had started digging furiously in the ground with his hands. He was not sure if he was digging up Stanley or the drugs. Arno was still holding the knife and was only a few feet away. Suddenly the sound of two explosions and gunfire startled both of them. Arno could not help but turn to look in the direction of the gunfire. Ron knew it was now or never. He reached around and pulled the small .380 pistol from his pocket and jacked a round into the receiver. From his many visits to a shooting range in Cleveland, he was very knowledgeable about handguns, but he had never fired this weapon and did not know if it would even work. He pointed at Arno's center of mass. Arno turned and saw the gun pointed at him. He rushed forward with the knife raised, figuring the little man would not shoot. Ron did not hesitate and emptied the magazine from the small pistol into Arno's chest. Arno fell to his knees only two feet from Ron. Arno looked at his chest and saw blood spurting from several holes. He looked at Ron with a puzzled expression.

"How . . . ?" Arno croaked, wondering where the small pistol had come from. "I used to do a lot of shooting, asshole." Ron hissed.

Arno's eyes closed and then he fell forward, face first in the sand. The knife was still in his hand. Ron got up slowly. He was still scared and his adrenalin rush made him shake. He was not sure Arno was down for sure. He nudged the body with his foot, still holding the empty pistol as if it could still fire. He turned the body over and saw that he had punched four holes in the man's chest. Arno was not breathing. Ron kicked the knife away and pulled the Uzi from the corpse. Now he had an Uzi. He had never fired one of these but it was a simple weapon. Ron walked over to the near palm tree and sat on the sand. He was so nervous he dropped the empty pistol. He could still hear shooting on the other side of the island but it suddenly stopped. Then he saw a helicopter fly over his position. He could see the pilot and the pilot saw him as their eyes met. The helicopter had a US Navy insignia on it. Ron wondered just what the hell was happening. The helicopter did not stop but flew away to the east.

Ron remembered that Stanley had a .38 caliber revolver that he had buried near the tree. He wondered if it still worked after all the rain and storm from the previous night. He dug in the sand and found the weapon. It appeared to be dry and was loaded with four rounds. He took the revolver and the Uzi and started to walk back down to the camp site. He was still in the underbrush near the camp when he looked over and saw Sara sneaking up on Uri with a piece of driftwood in her hands. Uri was facing the lagoon, watching the fireworks. The shooting had stopped and the quiet was ominous. Ron did not have time to warn her to stop as she hit Uri hard with the driftwood. The piece broke on Uri's head and Sara fell forward to her hands on the sand. Uri staggered a few paces, holding his hand to his head. Uri turned to Sara. Ron rushed toward them, dropping the Uzi but cocking the revolver. He knew hand guns and there was no time to learn how to shoot the Uzi.

"You Bitch!" Uri screamed as he raised the Uzi to shoot her. Sara knew then that she was going to die.

"Hey!" Ron yelled at Uri as he emerged from the bushes about 10 yards away.

Ron pointed the revolver at Uri.

"You! . . . " Uri swung around with the Uzi pointing it at Ron but he was not fast enough as Ron shot him in the solar plexus twice with the revolver. Uri dropped the Uzi and fell backward. Sara looked at Ron with a look of relief on her face.

"We were afraid they were going to kill you." she said, tears running down her face. She got up and ran to him, hugging him.

On the boat Chino and Caputo had killed as many of the French sailors as they could. They knew that Captain Bourne, his engine mechanic and Navigator had all jumped overboard on the side opposite the yacht and were swimming to the other side of the atoll. Caputo was not worried about them right now. He would deal with them later. They would have to pay for killing Huwala. Just then he heard the two pistol shots from the beach as Ron killed Uri. He turned to Chino.

"We better get over there." Caputo commanded Chino.

Ron looked out into the lagoon. It looked like a boat was burning and sinking in the lagoon. It had a red stripe on the bow as many coast guard cutters typically had. But it was on fire and sinking now. A large plume of black smoke rose over the stricken vessel. He saw Caputo and Chino get into their small boat and start the engine. They were both holding Uzis. He turned to Sara. He now had two Uzis and a pistol with two bullets.

"Sara. Please go hide with the other girls in the trees." He gave her the .38 pistol. "Do you know how to use this?

"I grew up in Pennsylvania on a farm. We used guns. You just pull the trigger right?" Sara replied. She wanted to stay with Ron, but he wanted her away from the confrontation with Caputo. She quickly kissed him on the mouth and reluctantly ran back into the trees.

"Go." Ron was shocked by the kiss but could not take the time to worry about it. He looked at the Uzi. He had to figure out how it worked but did not have much time. He pulled back the priming knob on the top of the gun. A bullet was ejected. Wow, it was ready to fire. He saw a lever on the side of the weapon. There were three positions marked with Israeli symbols. He assumed that the one farthest back was the "Safe", the second position to single fire and the one left to be for fully automatic. It was in the third position, so he kept it there. He was not sure how many rounds these guns held but thought it was about 20. He went over and crouched behind the big rock near his cooking fire spot. Although he had never fired an Uzi he had read about them. It was an Israeli manufactured weapon and tended to pull up and to the right as it was fired. So, he would start pointing at the left of his target and let the weapon traverse to the right. The handle of the gun had a pressure release to allow it to fire. He had seen the similar mechanism on some Colt weapons he had shot at the range. He hoped he was quick enough to get them. He had the element of surprise but these guys were professionals.

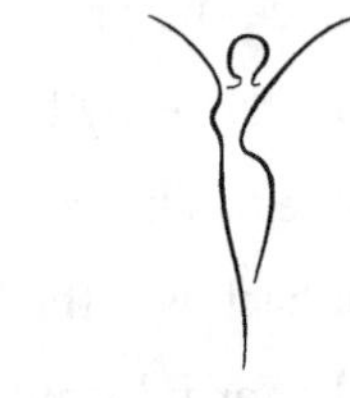

Chapter 75
Day 7   4:45 PM

The boat containing Caputo and Chino was approaching. Caputo was concerned, hearing Ron's shots killing Uri. Caputo and Chino got out of the boat; their guns ready. Caputo looked around for Uri and the girls.

"Uri . . . where are you?" Caputo shouted as he came nearer to the campsite. Chino sensed something was wrong. Uri would have greeted them at the shore. He had not taken time to reload his gun but figured he still had at least five rounds in his Uzi. He was just thinking about replacing the magazine when Ron popped up from behind the rock.

Ron did not hesitate this time. He stood up and fired the Uzi at both Chino and Caputo, hitting them both several times. Chino managed to get off a quick burst at Ron as he fell down. Several of Chino's rounds hit the rock and Ron felt a sharp sting in his left arm but kept firing at both of them until the magazine was empty. The quiet following all of the shooting was total. Ron was sure he had killed them both but had to make sure. He walked toward the bodies. Chino was definitely dead with four shots in his chest. Caputo was still breathing. He opened his eyes and looked at Ron. He had been shot at least three times with at least one fatal wound. He had thrown his hands up when he was shot and his Uzi had fallen behind him. He was lying on the ground with blood spurting from an artery in his neck.

He was struggling to get his pistol out of his holster but stopped when he saw Ron standing over him.

"What are you?" he asked looking at Ron with a rasping breath. He wondered if the man was a policeman or FBI agent.

"Just an engineer." Ron answered, looking at Caputo.

"Well ahhhhh." Caputo muttered as he turned his head in death.

Betty came running up to him. "Are they….?" she asked still frightened.

"Yes. I guess I killed them." Ron was feeling giddy. He was not happy to have killed the men, but he was just so relieved that he had actually survived. He had been in a shooting club back in Cleveland which was why he was able to use the weapons so well. Still, in all of the years of simple target practice he had never thought he would be capable or have to shoot an actual person.

Sara walked up, still holding the pistol. She looked at Ron in amazement. This quite-mannered, gentle man had just killed three of the toughest gangsters she had ever seen and appeared to be ok with it. Then she saw he was bleeding badly from his arm.

"You are hurt," she said to him, pointing at his arm.

"Owww," he said as he felt real pain for the first time. "It looks like he got me too." But it was only a flesh wound. One of the 9mm bullets from Chino's Uzi had plowed a furrow through his outer bicep. A few more inches to the right and it would have punctured him in the heart. He sat down on the sand. Blood was pouring down his arm. He was starting to feel light headed. He figured he was going into shock. Sara ran to get something to stem the blood flow. Taylor and Sylvia came out of the woods. They were shocked to see all of the bloody carnage.

"Wow. You . . . you did all this?" Taylor asked Ron with wide eyes.

"Yeah . . . I couldn't let them take you as a hostage. They would have eventually killed you. That is what these types do to hostages so they won't get identified later." Ron was starting to run off at the mouth. The shock of everything was starting to get to him. He decided to be quiet before he began to babble any more.

Betty turned to Ron. "Are you an agent for the FBI or something?" Betty asked looking at all of the bloodshed.

Ron looked at her. "No, I am just a plain old engineer." He was definitely getting weaker now. His words were slurring a bit. Sara came over with one of her cotton dresses and tore a long piece of it off. She wound it around the wound on his arm and pinned it with a safety pin. It turned red almost immediately but it was slowing the blood seepage.

Just then, a large Navy ship entered the lagoon. It was many times larger than the French coast guard cutter or the gangster's yacht. It pulled up between the burning hulk of the coast guard cutter and the yacht. It was the USS Preble. With several of the Navy guns trained on the yacht, a man on the Preble's bridge with a loudspeaker shouted to the yacht, "Give yourselves up or I will blow your boat out of the water." Randy threw his AR-15 into the water. He and Arturo walked out of the cabin with their hands up. They knew it was useless to resist now. Captain Bourn and his two remaining crewmen swam over to the naval ship and were helped aboard. Captain Bourne asked to talk to the captain and was helped to the bridge to talk with Captain Anderson.

Captain Anderson turned to Bourne as he arrived. "Hello Captain, welcome aboard. It looks like your ship has been badly damaged." Captain Bourne had been given a towel to dry off.

"They caught us by surprise." Bourne said sadly.

"Hello, Captain." Lieutenant Olsen greeted the French commander. "I saw them shoot your ship from my helicopter. It looked like they were using some sort of artillery."

"Yes. We were not prepared for it. The leader is on shore with the survivors. You better send a party over to rescue them. His name is Caputo and he is the toughest, most ruthless pirate of these islands. He just killed most of my crew."

"So, did you see some survivors?" Anderson asked Olsen.

"I saw several women near the lagoon being held at gunpoint on the beach and at least one man on the other side of the island." Olsen recalled.

"Ok. I will organize a combat party and go ashore. There was at least a platoon of marines on his boat. It was time for them to earn their pay. He gave orders for the marines to form up a group of six men with full combat armor and weapons to be ready to disembark in five minutes. He himself went to his cabin and retrieved his pistol. Both Captain Bourne and Olsen insisted on going along so he said OK. Captain Anderson and Olsen put on their combat flak jackets and handed one to Captain Bourne who put it on. They then climbed into the boat with the six marines. The marine, Sargent Harold Cook looked over at the captain and asked: "You sure you want to go with us sir? The French guy said these were terrible hardened criminals and that it is very likely that we will have to defend ourselves."

"That's ok, Sargent. This Caputo Guy will probably try to hold the women as hostages and I intend to be the one doing the negotiating," Captain Anderson replied.

They got into the launch and first headed to the yacht where two of the marines got off to secure it. Once Captain Anderson was assured that there were no other bandits hiding on board and the two remaining outlaws were handcuffed, he had the launch go to the beach and land next to Caputo's outboard. The four marines got off first with their MP5 automatic weapons at the ready. They moved forward cautiously, crouching low. When they approached the campsite they found what was left of Caputo and Chino. Then they saw a smaller man sitting on the ground who was obviously bleeding but with four women dressed in bikinis surrounding him. There was an Uzi in front of him and Sargent Cook walked over, kicked the Uzi away and pointed his weapon at Ron. Sara got up and stood between the Sargent and Ron.

"Put that weapon down!" she commanded. "Ron is our hero. He saved us from these awful men."

The Sargent took a couple of steps backward, unprepared for this woman's fury. So, the man sitting on the ground must be a good guy, he thought. Captain Bourne and Captain Anderson walked up and saw the bullet-riddled corpses of Caputo and Chino. Bourne turned to Captain Anderson.

"This man is the most feared criminal leader in all of the islands!" he said pointing to Caputo. "And this one . . . He is a known expert brutal assassin killer who has been wanted for quite some time. People are scared just to hear his name," he pointed to Chino.

Captain Anderson looked at the two corpses. "Apparently he was not good enough this time." They walked up to the cluster of women. Sargent Cook turned to Captain Anderson.

"The women say the guy sitting over there is the one who saved them." He pointed to Ron. "We found another bad guy over in those bushes to the right and another one at the top of the hill. So that makes four he shot to death." The Sargent was apparently impressed.

"Ok Sargent. Thank you. Please check out the rest of the area just to make sure". Captain Anderson and Captain Bourne approached the group of women. Olsen had already run over and was having a conversation with Taylor. He was telling her he was a big fan and wanted her autograph. She was smiling broadly at him and obviously was happy to meet him. The man Ron, was sitting on the sand. It looked like he had lost a lot of blood from the wound on his arm. Captain Bourne approached Ron.

"You killed all these men?" Bourne was amazed. He knew that men like Chino were almost never caught off guard.

"I guess so," Ron replied looking at the man in the wet French uniform. "Lieutenant Olsen!" Captain Anderson called.

"Yes sir." Olsen turned to his captain.

"Contact the ship; have them send over a medic immediately. This man has been hurt." He turned back to Ron and the ladies in their colorful bikinis. Olsen ran back to the launch.

Anderson turned to Ron. "I will have to take you into custody until we make a full investigation." he told Ron.

"You will do nothing of the sort!" Taylor stood up in front of the captain. "This man has done nothing except to find us shelter, food and water for a week and now just saved us from these terrible men. I will not have you treat him as a criminal!" She shoved her index finger into his chest. She was obviously not impressed by his Navy uniform.

"But . . . " Captain Anderson was stunned. He recognized the famous singer and knew she was a powerful woman. And she looked very determined, even only wearing a bikini.

"OK . . . OK, but I will need you all to fill out a statement about what happened here." He looked at Ron. Wow. Here was a guy that had been stranded on an island for a whole week alone with four beautiful sexy women. Apparently he had forged a strong bond with these women.

Chapter 76
Day 7   5:45 PM

The women had gathered up as much of their clothing as they could and put on enough so as not to excite the navy men on the ship. Walking around a navy ship in bikinis was sure to distract the men. The ship's medic had examined Sylvia's arm when he came ashore and was amazed that it had been set perfectly and was knitting nicely.

"Who set your arm?" He asked.

"Ron did it the first day we were here," she replied.

That brought a raising of eyebrows from Captain Anderson who overheard the conversation.

Captain Anderson was watching as his men escorted the women toward the launch.

A medic had bandaged Ron's arm and was preparing to take him back to the ship. "Wait." Ron shouted as the medic helped him up.

"What is it now?" Anderson asked.

"I have to get my wife!" Ron struggled against the medic's grip.

"Your wife?" Captain Anderson asked stunned. Was there another woman on the island? That was not possible; his men had searched thoroughly and had not found anyone else on the Atoll.

Sara dropped her suitcase and ran over to them. "I know where she is!" She ran over to the bushes where Ron often sat in the evenings looking at the urn. She grabbed it and ran back to them. "Here she is." She handed the urn to Ron. Ron grabbed the urn and held it to his chest. Tears were flowing down his cheek. "Thank you," he looked at Sara. She was starting to cry also, the day's events finally getting to her. She hugged Ron and he hugged her back. Even Taylor started to cry, watching them.

Captain Anderson was curious but did not say anything. It looked like the funeral urn was the only possession Ron cared about.

"Do you have any food on that boat? We missed our fish dinner tonight with all of the excitement." Betty asked Captain Anderson.

"Sure. We have a fully stocked galley. You can order anything you want once we get back. If you want fish, we have that too."

Betty looked at him with a frown. "I never want to eat fish ever again." She turned to walk to the launch.

"I want to take shower first!" Taylor shouted as she ran to the launch. "'Me too," added Sylvia

Well…let's all get back to the ship." His men had buried the dead French soldiers, and Caputo and his men in shallow graves. They would be exhumed at a later date. Right now, it was imperative to get the survivors back to Papeete where there were better medical facilities to examine the survivors. He assigned Captain Bourne the task of getting the pirate yacht back to port with his two men. He knew that Bourne would be able to confiscate the vessel as salvage. But it was the least Captain Anderson could do since his Coast Guard cutter had finally sunk in the lagoon. Besides, Captain Bourne would have to explain the loss of his vessel. Captain Anderson had assigned two marines to help Captain Bourne with the yacht.

"Captain Bourne." He turned to the Frenchman. "Please keep the news of the rescued survivors quiet until we get back to Papeete. I don't want to be met by a hundred reporters at the dock."

"I understand, Captain Anderson. I will maintain radio silence as I follow you in the yacht." He looked at the two armed marines that were going to assist him with the yacht. Although the US Navy had captured the yacht, Captain Anderson had informed him that it was French property and would not attempt to claim salvage rights. So, he would benefit. The best thing was that the criminal Caputo and his gang had been eliminated, so he was happy.

CHAPTER 77
DAY 7   6:30 PM

Everyone was back on board the USS Preble. The women had been able to take their showers and were all dressed in more conservative travel clothing. Ron had been given a fresh set of sailor fatigues and an undershirt to replace his sweat-stained shorts and T-shirt. Word had gotten out by the marines that Ron had single handedly killed four of the criminals and the sailors treated him with a lot of respect. The survivors were all ordered and escorted to the ward room on the Preble for debriefing. The ship had left the atoll and had set course for Papeete. They were not moving at flank speed since Caputo's old yacht was trying to follow the warship. The executive officer was on the bridge running the ship. Captain Anderson, Lieutenant Olsen, Sargent Cook and Ensign Owens were sitting around the ward room table waiting for the survivors to join them. Captain Anderson sat at the head of the table, his officers sitting on the long side of the table with Ensign Owens sitting adjacent to the captain, and Sargent Cook sitting at the far end near the door. Ensign Owens had a laptop and opened it. He was going to record the debriefing. A video camera was positioned behind Captain Anderson and the Ensign got up to turn it on. One by one the survivors filed in and sat on the opposite side of the table, facing the Navy men. Taylor entered first and sat by Captain Anderson, followed by her mother

Sara, Betty and Sylvia in that order. Ron Pritchard was the last to enter and sat at the end of the table facing Captain Anderson.

"Sorry to interrupt your acclimation back to civilization, but I must debrief you before I report to the Admiral that you have been found. I have to have answers for potential questions he may ask." A ship steward entered the room. "I know you have not had time to eat yet so you may tell the steward what you want and he will bring it in here for you while we talk."

Betty immediately blurted out "I want a cheeseburger and fries and a pot of coffee." Taylor and her mother ordered the same but with a soft drink. Sylvia asked if she could have chicken salad with a fruit plate and a cranberry juice. That left Ron who quietly also ordered a cheeseburger but with two beers. The steward wrote down the order and left.

"Now that we have that taken care of, I have some questions." Captain Anderson looked at Ron. "I understand that you discovered that the pilot had passed out and the plane was flying past its destination."

"We all fell asleep in the passenger cabin. When I woke up and looked at the time I knew something was wrong. I awoke Stan and we went into the cockpit. The pilot was dead. He had no pulse." Ron looked at him plainly. He knew there were questions to be answered but he was tired and it showed.

"Stanley was the body guard that was killed by a shark?" Anderson asked.

"Yes. The plane ran out of fuel as we approached the island. I tried to get it to land in the lagoon but we hit the reef hard and sort of bounced into the lagoon," Ron explained. "Stan hit his head on the console and was unconscious and bleeding slightly. The plane was sinking so we all had swim for it. He was unconscious so I had to put the life preserver on him and tow him ashore. About half way to the beach we were attacked by sharks. I managed to kick a couple of them away but one got Stan. It was raining pretty hard and was dark. I did not see he was hurt until we reached the beach."

"So, you were flying the plane?" Anderson asked.

"I had a couple of lessons in a Cessna. Nobody else wanted to try." Ron responded.

"But there was a life raft, why not use it?" Anderson asked.

"The inflator tank was corroded and empty. I just threw the raft in the water but it drifted toward shore before I could get Stan on it." Ron was feeling bad now.

"Ok. So, you got to shore and he was dead?"

"He was still breathing but had lost a lot of blood. I tied a tourniquet on his leg above where the shark had bitten him. I think the major leg artery had been cut" Ron explained. "I did find the life raft on the shore and tried my best to rig a tent to keep everyone out of the rain. We huddled under it that night. In the morning Stan was not breathing, so I took him up the hill and buried him." Ron was visibly getting tired.

Captain Anderson turned to Taylor. "The medical officer said that you all were in pretty good shape. How did you stay alive for seven days?"

"We ate fish, crabs, shark and coconuts," Taylor said. "Ron caught the fish and cooked it for us. He showed us how to eat the coconuts. He also found a pool of water that was left over from the storm."

"You all swam from the sinking plane, yet you had your suitcases?"

"The next day Ron swam back to the plane and retrieved those for us," Sara answered. He avoided the sharks in the daylight."

"You went back into shark-infested water for their suitcases?" Anderson addressed Ron.

"The plane had sunk so that it was perpendicular in the water with the one float holding it to the surface. So, there was some air trapped in the cabin. I could get a breath or two between each suitcase. I just had to find the one that had my wife's ashes in it.

"Yes. Tell me about that." Anderson asked.

"My wife died of cancer last December. She had always wanted to go to Tahiti. So, since we had already booked a trip to go to Bora Bora before she died, I brought her ashes out here to spread on the sand in Bora Bora. It was her last dying wish." Ron looked down at the table.

"You made a special trip just to spread your dead wife's ashes on the beach?" Captain Anderson asked incredulously.

"I know it sounds pretty stupid now but….I did not know how else to fulfill her wish."

Just then the steward entered with a cart holding the food they had ordered.

There was a pause as the women dug into their food as if they were starving. Ron picked up the cheeseburger and set it back down. He grabbed a can of beer and opened it. He drank it down without stopping. Then he started to eat the cheeseburger.

Captain Anderson resumed the interrogation. "Tell me about earlier today when the pirates came." Betty paused from her meal and answered.

"We were sitting in the shade waiting for Ron and Taylor to return with the water bottles from the eastern island when the yacht entered the lagoon. We all thought we were being saved, but that terrible little man and his hoodlums only wanted to capture Taylor and hold her for ransom. They said they were going to sell Sylvia and me to the sex slave trade," Betty exclaimed.

"They also were looking for their drugs. Apparently they were shipping heroin on the charter plane." Sara noted.

"Drugs?" The captain asked.

Taylor spoke up. "Yes. When Ron was rescuing our clothes he found a large bag of what looked like drugs. He hid it under some bushes and then later buried it near Stan's grave." she answered.

"I didn't know about that." Sara said.

"Ron didn't want anyone else to know about it so he quietly buried it." Taylor said.

Sara continued: "When Ron came back with Taylor, they threatened to shoot me if Ron didn't give them back the drugs. So, Ron led the big ugly guy up the hill to dig up the drugs. I heard the short fat guy say to the big guy to use the knife on Ron so as not to disturb the rest of us." Sara related. "I knew then that he was going to kill Ron after getting the drugs."

Captain Anderson looked at Ron. "How did you get out of that?'

"Well, I was digging to get the drugs when we heard some explosions. The big man turned to look down the hill so I took out the small pistol that I had taken off of Teddy and shot the big guy," Ron related.

"Teddy was the dead pilot?"

"Yes. I had to search his pockets to find the key to the luggage compartment and found a small .380 pistol. I shoved it in my pocket, thinking it might come in handy, maybe to kill a shark. Those men never bothered to search me; they must have assumed that we were all defenseless," Ron told Anderson.

"So, then you killed the other three gangsters?"

"With all of the shooting in the lagoon between the Coast Guard boat and the yacht, the guy left behind to guard the women turned to watch the action. Sara took a piece of driftwood and snuck up on him, and hit him on the head. He turned to shoot her so I rushed out of the bushes and shot him. When the other goons came back to the beach I shot them with an Uzi I took off the dead guy." Ron was shaking a little bit, remembering the killing. "I have practiced shooting at the range a lot, but never thought I would have to kill someone." He looked down at the table again.

"Ron didn't have any choice. It was us or them." Sara interjected. "He is my hero."

"Wow. That is quite some story. You must be a Hero. You were with four sexy women for a week and never had any relations with them?" Captain Anderson said unbelieving.

"He was a perfect gentleman with us!" Betty and Sylvia both said together.

"That is not entirely true." Ron said. "I did fall in love with Sara but we didn't do anything but kiss once."

Captain Anderson was amazed. Here was a middle-aged man stuck on an island who provided food, shelter and protection for a bunch of women and never asked for anything in return.

"Just what do you do back home?" Anderson was curious. "I am just an engineer," Ron answered.

"Well, you deserve a medal for your actions against those criminals." Anderson ended the debriefing. He did turn to Taylor and whispered in her ear. "If possible, could you sing a couple of songs for the men tonight? We have one of your records we could play on the loudspeaker."

"I guess I could," Taylor replied.

CHAPTER 78
DAY 7   9:00 PM

With most of the ships' company (except essential persons running the ship) sitting on the aft helicopter deck, Taylor Smith stood on the deck above and performed three songs from one of her albums. She of course, was wearing one of her sexy show costumes that had managed to survive the island ordeal. Every one cheered and clapped loudly. Afterward she signed autographs for anyone that wanted one. Betty, Sara and Sylvia sat among the crowd watching Taylor dance around the deck as she sang. It was a good show and everyone enjoyed it. Ron had stayed in the cabin that they had let him share with Ensign Owens. He had fallen asleep clutching the funeral urn on a cot they had set up. He was completely exhausted from the day's ordeal.

Chapter 79
Day 8   8:00 AM

The USS Preble entered the harbor at Papeete to dock. Captain Anderson had finally called the Admiral back at Pearl and reported that the survivors had been found and were in good health. He had a full report that he was sending. The Admiral was elated and congratulated Anderson on a good job.

Anderson had also called the US and French Consulates and asked them to be at the dock to meet the ship. He noticed a lack of reporters so was somewhat relieved. As Taylor and her mother departed the ship, Captain Anderson introduced Taylor to the Consulates, who were very happy to meet her. The French Consul had made arrangements for the survivors to stay at the best hotel, which was right near the airport. The French Consul noted that Taylor's fiancé was staying at that same hotel. Should he call ahead and warn him that she was coming? "No," she replied, she wanted to surprise him. The long absence from him and the experience of the past week had softened her feelings for him and she wanted to make love with him. As they left the ship, Ron turned to Betty and said: "Well, we are back where we all started," he joked.

"Yes, but it is so good to be back to civilization." She had lost her cell phone on the island and could not wait to get one so she could get on Facebook. Somehow it was not quite as important as it once would have been. Sylvia followed the rest, her arm in a sling. She had to call the producer for the photo shoot to see if it was still possible to do. Sara slowed to walk with Ron. "Well, we are back. Was it true when you said you loved me?" she asked.

"Yes. I want to be with you, if you will have me." He looked in her eyes. "Why don't you come to my room once we are settled in?"

"I would love to, but I have to do something first." He was holding the urn. "I understand. Would you let me help you?"

"Yes. That would be nice," he replied.

They all piled into a long black limousine that would take them to the hotel. Taylor turned to her mother who was sitting next to Ron and handed her a credit card. Looking at Ron in his navy fatigues, she said: "Take him out to buy whatever he wants for clothing and travel stuff. It's on me."

Chapter 80
Day 8 9:30 AM

The group had arrived at the Hotel. The word was finally out that Taylor Smith was found alive. So, a throng of reporters who were at the hotel started taking her picture the minute she arrived. She basically ignored them and told them she would meet them in a few minutes in a nearby conference room to answer questions once she had checked in. That appeared to satisfy them for the moment. As she checked in, she asked which room her fiancé was in. The clerk, impressed to be talking to such an important celebrity told her the room number. She walked up the stairs to her floor. Betty was with her but Taylor handed her key to Betty and told her she would be a few minutes. She walked down the hall to Steve's room and knocked on his door.

Steve Hariman was sitting in a robe on his couch. He was exhausted from another erotic night with Suzy. He had just picked up the phone to order some breakfast from room service when he heard the knock on his door. He had not yet turned on his phone or the TV, so he had not heard the news flash that Taylor Smith had been found alive and was in Papeete. He walked over to the door. He was shocked to see Taylor standing there.

Taylor rushed in and hugged him. She was about to kiss him when the door to the bathroom opened and Suzy came out drying her hair with a towel. She had a towel wrapped around her waist but was otherwise naked. She had the hair towel in her eyes so she did not notice the door was open.

"Stevie, please have room service order more towels," she said. "We have used these all up."

Taylor looked over and saw Suzy and was shocked. "You Bastard!" she screamed at him. Steve just stumbled backward a couple of steps. He was stunned.

"You are alive!" he shouted. "It's a miracle!"

"Oh my god." Suzy said when she saw Taylor Smith standing there. She tried to cover up best she could but the towel at her waist dropped, leaving her completely naked. Just then a reporter entered the open door and took a couple of pictures. Taylor turned to hit him but he ducked out of the door and ran down the hall shouting "I got it…. I got it."

"We are through." Taylor said to Steve coldly and turned and walked out the door.

Steve wanted to run after her but he was naked under his robe. He turned to Suzy. "Look what you have done to me, you little bitch."

"Yeah, as if you didn't enjoy it," Suzy replied. She calmly got into her clothes and then walked out the door without saying another word.

Steve sat back down on the couch, his head in his hands. *What was he going to do now?* he wondered.

CHAPTER 80
DAY 9   10:00 AM

Sylvia was on the phone to Franklin Carrere in Bora Bora about the photo shoot. "Sylvia, half my people already went home. It will take a week to get them back.

You already owe me thousands of dollars for the incurred overhead from last week. We can't possibly do it this week," he pleaded.

"Ok Frank, call them back. We will double the contract value and absorb your overhead," Sylvia commanded. Taylor was in a spending mood and told Sylvia she still wanted to do the shoot in Bora Bora.

"Really? Well, I suppose we could make the arrangements for the end of the week. How does that sound?" Frank was relieved. He could sell that deal to his boss.

"That's fine Frank. Taylor needs a few days to rest up anyway."

"That must have been a terrible ordeal she, ah…you both went through." Frank had read the story in the newspapers and was amazed. "Just who was that guy with you on the island? His name wasn't in the paper," he asked.

"He is just a middle-aged man who doesn't want the publicity," she replied. "Well, Taylor made him out to be a real hero . . . I just wondered."

"If it wasn't for him, we wouldn't have survived. That is all you need to know." Sylvia was surprised that Ron did not want the publicity. He was a strange guy, saving their lives, taking care of them on the island and killing the gangsters.

"Ok, send over the contract and I will start the ball rolling," Frank replied.

Sylvia hung up the phone. Her arm was still in a cast. She dictated the terms of the new contract to her secretary back in Los Angles. It would be transmitted back today and she would send it over to Frank for his review. It was funny, they had left Papeete with the intention of shooting the music video on Bora Bora and here they were back on Papeete. She wondered if they ever would get to see Bora Bora.

CHAPTER 81
DAY 9   11:00 AM

Sara and Ron were walking along a public beach near the Papeete Airport. They had spent the morning buying him a new wardrobe and some personal items all on Taylor's credit card. Ron felt a little weird about letting Taylor do this for him but she had insisted. He had settled for a modest pair of jeans and a couple of polo shirts. He selected one the same color as the blue summer dress Sara was wearing. He had left almost everything he brought with him on the island but he still had the urn in his hands. Sara was with him. They had sat on a bench and argued that Papeete was actually Tahiti, so technically even though it was not a resort at Bora Bora, it had a Tahitian beach. So, they walked along the shore, and when they were sure no one was watching she helped him spread the ashes along the beach near the water. The waves covered the ashes and took them out to sea. Once the urn was empty, Ron turned to Sara and they kissed.

"Thank you for helping." He had tears in his eyes. "Thank you for letting me help." Sara replied.

"Can I buy you lunch back at the hotel?" he asked.

"Sure." She replied. They walked back to the hotel holding hands. Ron deposited the urn in a waste basket and they went into the hotel to eat. They went into the restaurant and found a table near a window overlooking the ocean. They had a light meal and started to talk. Sara noticed that he had removed his wedding ring.

"Taylor says you can come with us to Bora Bora for the photo shoot," Sara started. "She sort of coerced the resort to renew our rooms for the photo shoot. You are more than welcome."

"I would like to, but I have already used up more vacation time than I had allocated. I have to return to Cleveland to go back to work." Ron stated.

"Please, I really wish you would reconsider." Sara started to beg.

"I have this feeling that I am fated never to see Bora Bora. I have had more than enough excitement on this trip. I am hoping that when you return to the states maybe we can get together sometime." Ron explained. He really hoped that Sara would visit him in Cleveland.

"I would like that," Sara stated. "I have something in my room I have to give you.

Can you please come up?" She asked.

"Sure," he agreed, wondering what this was about.

They got to her room and she closed the door. She went into the bedroom and said "It's in here." He followed her and she turned around and dropped her dress on the floor. She was wearing the skimpy blue bikini swim suit.

"Remember you said you would like to remove these?" she said huskily.

"God, you are beautiful," he whispered. He turned and closed the bedroom door and they headed to the bed and he did remove her bikini. He also undressed. They rolled on the bed and made love for the first time. Neither of them had done this since their spouses had died. It was sort of special. Afterward she cuddled with him.

"You are a gentle lover," Sara sighed. "I sort of thought you would be."

"I hope you enjoyed it as much as I did," Ron whispered in her ear. She answered him by passionately kissing him on the mouth.

CHAPTER 82
DAY 10

Ron was getting ready to board the flight back to Hawaii. Sara was with him to see him off. She and Taylor and the rest of her group were flying over to Bora Bora on a different commercial flight. Taylor had walked up to them in the terminal and thanked Ron again for saving her life. She saw the way her mother and Ron looked at each other and smiled.

"I hope you have a safe trip home," she said to Ron. "You must come and visit us in Tennessee some time." She blew him a kiss and walked away to join her group. Sara and Ron kissed once more, a tear forming on her cheek.

"I am going to miss you," she said sadly.

"I know. I will miss you too," Ron replied. His plane was boarding. Sylvia had arranged that he have first class flights all the way back to Cleveland. He turned to leave when Betty came running up and gave him a hug and a kiss on the cheek.

"I had to say goodbye and thank you one more time," she said excitedly. "I am glad to see you again," he replied. "Please have a good life."

"We owe you a lot," Betty whispered to him. "Please take care of yourself." "Have you ever known me not take care of things? "

"No, I guess not. Goodbye." Betty turned and walked away.

Ron turned again to Sara. "Goodbye." He turned walked up to the gate. He turned to look back at her and could see she was watching him leave with tears in her eyes. He got on the plane and took his seat. Life back home was never going to be the same, he thought.

Chapter 82
March

It was a real shock to return to snow-covered Cleveland after being in the tropics so long. Ron had acquired a deep tan that looked out of place among all of the other people at Hopkins Airport. His Honda was still at the park and fly place even though it had been parked a lot longer than he typically left it. At least they had not towed it away to an impound lot. The drive home was normal, although it felt different somehow. He got back in the house and turned the thermostat up. He was not used to the cold. He called work and apologized for taking more vacation days than he had signed up for. He explained that he had trouble getting travel arrangements after losing his wallet. He had to get a new passport at the US Consulate in Tahiti. His boss accepted that and was glad he was back since the project had stalled while he was away. He had a huge pile of mail and bills to go through. He looked through the newspapers and found the one announcing that Taylor Smith had been found. He scanned the story but did not see his name anywhere. He was glad. They had accepted his desire to be anonymous. He had enough excitement on the trip and the fact that he had killed four men really bothered him. True, they were bad men and it had to be done, but he still felt bad. He felt bad enough to go to his wife's church on Sunday and quietly ask God's forgiveness. He was not a religious person but he did feel better after going. He called both of his daughters and told them he had returned from Tahiti. They asked him how the trip was; and he only said it was normal and boring. He was tempted to tell them about Sara but was not sure that he would ever see her again so he said nothing. He really missed Sara. He thought about her constantly. But she and her daughter were from a different world. He just hoped she was happy.

Ron returned to work. Everyone kidded him about his deep tan but he just smiled and said he had a good vacation. He got right to work on the project and managed to get it going forward again. He found that when he concentrated on work he did not think of Sara. So, he worked harder than before. Everybody on the design team noticed he was different though. He was not joking with them anymore and often stayed by himself during breaks or went outside to walk by himself. They knew he had lost his wife a few months ago so they attributed his change to the fact that he was still mourning. Ron stopped going to the shooting range and dropped out of the gun club. He could not stand to hold a weapon again. He locked up his guns in his gun safe and hid the key in a drawer near his bedside. He was having bad dreams at night, often about the Caputo guy coming after him or torturing Sara. He often took a sleeping pill before bed to sleep, hoping he could avoid the dreams. Ron had sent a couple of letters to Sara telling her about Cleveland and saying he missed her a lot. He thought of Sara frequently but she had not called or written to him. He figured she was no longer interested in him.

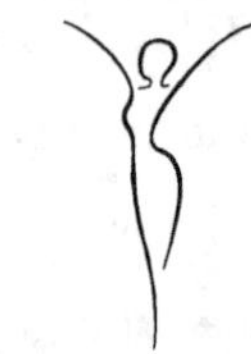

CHAPTER 83
APRIL

Ron Pritchard was home after a long day at work. He had just cooked and eaten a frozen meal and was cleaning up his kitchen. There was a knock at the front door. He looked at his watch. It was already 6:30. He wondered who it could be. He walked over to the door and opened it. There was a big black SUV in his driveway and two men dressed in dark suits were standing on his front porch. One was tall, the other slightly shorter. They were both young men, probably in their early thirties. They had the look of being military with short haircuts. Ron wondered what this was about.

"Are you Ron Pritchard?" The tall one asked. "Yes. How can I help you?" he asked,

"May we come in?" the tall man asked, showing his badge. It said he was FBI. "Sure, I guess so." Ron was concerned. What did the FBI want with him? Could it be about the men he killed? He stood back and let them in. They walked into his living room. "Sit down." He pointed to the couch while he walked over to his lounge chair, facing them. They all sat down.

"I am Special Agent Sam Stark, and this is John Russo of the Secret Service." The tall man said, pointing to his companion.

"What is this about?" Ron was starting to be concerned.

"You work as an aerospace engineer?" the shorter man finally spoke up.

"Yes." Ron responded, telling them where he worked. He started to think he must have done something wrong at work.

"You took a trip to Tahiti earlier this year?" The FBI man asked. "Yes," Ron answered.

"We read some transcripts of your actions there from a Navy report." The FBI man started. "It was a very interesting story." He sat further back on the couch, smiling. "It made you out to be a hero, saving some women from some dangerous criminals."

"I am no hero." Ron replied. "You must have me mixed up with someone else."

"I personally interviewed the rescued singer and her mother and they both said you saved their lives." The shorter man looked at him. "Are you denying you were there?"

Ron could see that he was not about to fool these men.

"OK, I was there, but I only did what I had to do. I just got lucky." He was starting to sweat. The two agents looked at each other. The Secret Service agent turned to Ron. "Ok then. We are here to tell you that a Navy Captain has nominated you for a Presidential Citation to be presented to you at the White House," the shorter man said, smiling. Ron was stunned. He was speechless. How could this be? "Well, what do you have to say about it?" The FBI agent asked. "No thanks. I can't do that." Ron managed to say.

"Why not?" The Secret Service man was amazed. No one ever turned down this type of honor.

"Look, I killed four men. It still bothers me. I can't accept any honor for doing that," Ron confessed.

"Are you sure? This is a big honor." The Secret Service man asked. "Yeah, I can't do this. I'm sorry." Ron looked down at the floor.

The two agents looked at each other. They both stood up. The FBI agent turned to Ron. "I read your file. It was a remarkable feat you accomplished.

I want to shake your hand." They shook hands. They turned to leave as Ron escorted them to the door. As he got to the door, the Secret Service man stopped to look back at Ron.

"I looked at your file. You didn't serve in the armed forces but you seemed to be well acquainted with the weapons you used."

"I used to shoot targets at the gun range quite frequently as a hobby," Ron explained.

"Interesting." he said as he walked out of the door. Both agents walked toward the black SUV that was parked in his driveway and got in. Ron watched them as they backed out and drove away. Ron closed the door and breathed a sigh of relief. He felt a little guilty for turning them down, but he just couldn't take the publicity that would result from accepting the citation. He went back in the kitchen and finished cleaning up. He began to think about Sara again. He supposed he wouldn't ever see her again. It was better to put it all behind him.

CHAPTER 84
MAY

Ron had just completed the special project at work. His boss was happy and the customer was happy. He had worked extra late shifts to get everything qualified by the deadline. His boss was aware of his effort and told him to take a few days off. Ron objected since there was another big project coming up. His boss insisted, and he finally gave in. On the way home he stopped to buy a six pack of beer. He had not had any since he had returned from Tahiti, but lately the bad dreams had finally stopped and he was beginning to feel comfortable again. He had been going to his wife's church somewhat frequently and had begun to think that everything was getting better with the passing of time. He got home and got a steak out of the freezer to grill. It was a nice warm day for May and he was going to take full advantage of it. He went out on the back porch and started the grill. He opened a beer and took a long drink. It really tasted good. He walked back inside to the kitchen to get some utensils. There was a knock on the door. He wondered who that could be. He opened the door. It was George Coleman.

"Hey Ron." George smiled at him. He was in a three piece suit. "George! How are you?" Ron answered.

"I was in the neighborhood and thought I would stop by." George came inside. "You want to stay for a steak? I just fired up the grill." Ron was really happy to see his friend.

"Twist my arm," George agreed, "You got any beer?"

"Sure, help yourself. There's some in the fridge," Ron replied he got another steak out of the freezer. "How is the new job with the Cleveland Police department?" he asked.

"It's really interesting. They have me working as a detective in the burglary division. We have solved a lot of theft cases already this year." George opened the beer and took a sip.

"How is Jen doing? Does she like living in Cleveland?" Ron asked.

"Yeah, she has a part interest in a flower shop and we have a nice bungalow on the west side. She is visiting her mother in Pittsburgh this week," George replied, "So, I thought I would stop over to see you."

"Well, I'm glad you did. Come on, we can sit out on the back porch." Ron grabbed the plate with the steaks.

Just then there was another knock on the door. Ron put down the plate.

"I wonder who that could be?" Ron said. He went to the door and opened it.

Sara Smith was standing there. She was wearing a blue dress and white sneakers. She had a suitcase in her hand. Ron was stunned.

"Hi Ron. I couldn't stay away any longer." She had tears in her eyes. "Do you still want me?"

"God, yes." He grabbed her and hugged her. "Please come inside." He pulled her into the house.

"I wasn't sure you . . . " she started. "Sara, I love you." Ron kissed her.

"Wow. Who is this?" George asked coming into the room.

Ron turned to face George. "George, this is Sara. We met in Tahiti." He turned to Sara and introduced George as his best friend. Sara smiled at George and said hello.

George looked at her again and recognized her. "Hey, wait a minute. Aren't you Sara Smith, Taylor Smith's mother? I remember seeing your picture in the paper when your daughter was rescued from that deserted island about a month ago." George remembered. Then he looked at Ron. "It was you!" he exclaimed. "You were the one that saved them. The papers talked about a man who saved them but never mentioned a name. Everybody wondered who it was." George was amazed.

"He did save us." Sara replied. "But he didn't want the publicity so we honored his wishes."

"Look, George . . . please keep this quiet, ok?" Ron pleaded. "Sure . . . but from what I read the guy was some sort of a hero."

"No, not a hero, I just helped out. Anyone would have done the same." Ron blushed.

"He is not just anyone, He saved our lives. And I am in love with him," Sara exclaimed, looking at Ron.

"Well, OK. I always wondered if you were involved in that mess when you went to Tahiti but you never said anything," George said.

"Hey, I was just about to grill some steaks. Will you join us?" He asked Sara, changing the subject.

"I always let you cook for me, remember?" Sara agreed.

Ron Grilled the steaks while Sara prepared a salad out of what she could find in Ron's refrigerator. While she was doing this and Ron was outside, George quizzed her on what actually happened on the island. When she told him all that Ron had done, he understood why Ron wanted to be anonymous. Ron did not care for fame or the attention that he would receive.

"That's the type of guy he is, he will do anything for you but doesn't want anybody else to know about it," George told her.

"Taylor made me stay in Tahiti with her for a month. She wanted to know if I really loved him or not. I couldn't wait to get back to him but I wasn't sure he still felt the same about me," Sara exclaimed.

George looked at her. "If he says he loves you then that means he really does.

He doesn't lie about things like that. It probably means he is totally committed to you."

Ron came in with the steaks and set the table. "I suppose she has been telling you a bunch of stuff about the island, but she tends to exaggerate," Ron informed George. Sara rolled her eyes at that but smiled at George and blinked her eyes. They had a great meal, and George told Sara about all of the trouble Ron got into when he was in college and George had to help him. They all had some good laughs. Later George left and Sara and Ron were finally alone. They moved to the front room and sat on the couch, sitting silently for a few minutes.

"Nice place you have here." Sara had to break the ice.

"I wrote you a couple of letters but you didn't write back," he said to Sara.

"Yes, I was in Tahiti with Taylor for a month and did not get them until I returned last week. I am sorry," Sara explained.

"That's OK. I've thought about you every day since we parted, but I wasn't sure you wanted to be with me," he told her, looking at the floor. "I know that sometimes when two people experience a violent drama together, they can become temporarily attached to each other and afterward when it is over, they lose that attachment," he explained.

"Ron, I know what type of man you are and I still love you." Sara looked at him seriously. "I am here to stay unless you kick me out." She looked intently at him.

"Wow. I must be one of the luckiest guys in the world. I want you to stay as long as you want." He leaned over and they kissed passionately.

THE END